FRIENDLY REMINDER

Last of all came the article that had cost him the most thought and care in selection. It was intended for Frances. After all, he acknowledged to himself, this was the gift in which he took the most pleasure. This was for his friend . . . his dearest. He drew his breath quickly as he dared to say it to himself and wondered what she would think if she knew he thought this way about her.

Then the eyes of the picture drew him irresistibly, and as he looked up, some queer twist of memory brought to his mind the song he had sung that evening: "I gave my life for thee, what hast thou given me?"

It came with startling clearness—and he sat down bewildered, all the pretty prideful gifts he had arrayed staring back reproachfully at him. . . .

THE FORGOTTEN FRIEND
AND OTHER STORIES

Living Books®
Tyndale House Publishers, Inc.
Wheaton, Illinois

This Tyndale House book
by Grace Livingston Hill
contains the complete text
of the original hardcover edition.
NOT ONE WORD
HAS BEEN OMITTED.

Living Books is a registered trademark of Tyndale House
Publishers, Inc.

Library of Congress Catalog Card Number 94-60937
ISBN 0-8423-1391-5

Printed in the United States of America

99 98 97 96 95 94
 6   5   4   3   2   1

CONTENTS

The Forgotten Friend

THE NIGHT was inky black and growing colder. Occasional dashes of rain brought a chill as it touched the faces of the hurrying pedestrians. The pavements gleamed black where the electric lights struck them, like children's slates just washed.

Gordon Pierce drew down his hat, turned up his collar, and dropped his umbrella a little lower to breast the gale, but just as he turned the corner into Church Street the uncertain wind caught the frail structure and twisted it inside out as if it had been a child's toy, and the hail pounded down Church Street rebounding from the stone steps of the church on the corner with such vengeance that the young man was fain to take refuge for the moment in the inviting open doorway till he could right himself or the severity of the storm should pass.

Hail storms are so unexpected that one cannot calculate upon them. This one lasted longer than was usual and pelted most unmercifully in at the doorway so that the refugee stepped further into the lighted entrance way of the church, taking off his hat to shake the hail stones from its brim.

As he did so his ear caught the sweet strains of the pipe organ within, and a rich tenor voice floated out faintly through the closed leather swinging doors from the lighted room beyond.

Gordon Pierce was fond of music and knew a fine voice when he heard it. This one attracted him. He stepped nearer and listened a moment, then stealthily pushed open the noiseless door and stepped inside the audience room.

There were only a few people in the brightly lighted church and they were gathered up toward the front near the pulpit and the choir gallery. The stranger stepped softly in and stood with hat in hand listening to the sweet music, then drawn irresistibly he moved silently a little further down the aisle to a seat somewhat behind the audience and sat down.

A prayer followed. Until then he had thought this a small private rehearsal for a favored few. Of course he could not go out during a prayer, and he bowed his head in annoyance that he had cornered himself in a religious meeting by coming so far forward, when he was extremely anxious to hasten home.

He was meditating a quiet flight as soon as the prayer should be over, when the same sweet voice that had first lured him in, broke the stillness that followed the petition. And this time it was a hymn that was sung. Yet the voice was insistent, clear, demanding attention.

> *"I gave my life for thee,*
> *My precious blood I shed*
> *That thou might'st ransomed be*
> *And quickened from the dead.*
> *I gave my life for thee,*
> *What hast thou given for me?"*

The words were so old, but to the young man they sounded new. It was as if the question had been asked of his own startled heart by an angel. He forgot about trying to slip out before the meeting went further on and listened.

The quiet faced man who stepped to the edge of the platform as the singer ceased and began to talk in a low but impressive voice was a missionary, but the unexpected listener did not know it. He would have been amazed beyond measure if he had known at that moment that he was to be enthralled with interest in a missionary meeting, but this was the case. It was not like any missionary meeting he had ever heard of before though, and he did not recognize it as such even after it was over and he had dropped the last fifty-cent piece his pockets contained into the collection basket with a feeling of annoyance that he had no more.

He had heard things that evening that stirred him deeply.

The storm had ceased when he picked his way out into the slippery streets now white with a fine sleet it had left as a parting salute. As he made his way thoughtfully to his boarding house his mind was still intent upon the new thoughts the speaker had left with him, but when he turned the lights on in his own room he saw a pile of paper parcels and boxes on the bed and floor which made him forget his evening experiences completely.

"Great Scott!" he ejaculated aloud, "did I

buy all those things? There'll be a howling big bill to pay when my next month's salary comes, and no mistake."

Then with the pleasure of a child he gave himself up to the investigation of his purchases.

Most of the things were Christmas presents he had that afternoon purchased for his friends and the various members of his family. He felt a deep sense of satisfaction in their fineness and beauty as he opened first one and then another. He had done the thing up fine this time as became a young man who was away from home in business for the first time in his life and getting what in the eyes of his family was an exceedingly large salary for one who had been a boy but the other day.

There was the silk dress for mother. He had always said he would buy his mother a silk dress when he got a chance, and he had saved for this for several months. He felt its rich shining folds with clumsy inexperienced fingers and shook it out in a lustrous heap over the bed to admire it. It was all right, for he had asked Frances to tell him just what was the suitable thing for his mother, and she had said black *peau de soie,* and he had carried samples for her inspection one evening when he called, and she had bent over them and studied and talked wisely of texture and wear while the soft light from the opal lamp shone on her pretty hair, and he had thought how sensible she was to advise for the medium price, even though her father was reported to be a millionaire. He smiled at the innocent silk on the bed as though it brought a vision of Frances.

For his sister Mildred he had bought Hoffman's boy head of Christ. He knew that she fancied this particular picture and wanted it. It wasn't exactly the picture he would have selected for her if she had not expressed a strong desire for it, but it was a pretty thing and he placed it on his mantel and surveyed it pleasantly and critically, and as he did so something in the frank, deep gaze of the boy in the picture reminded him of the strange meeting he had attended that evening and the new thoughts that had been stirred by it. Somehow a wave of compunction went through his conscience as he turned back to the new possessions on the bed and remembered the paltry fifty cents he had put in the collection plate.

Last of all of his purchases came the article which had cost him the most thought and care in selection. It was a delicate little bronze statue, fine of workmanship and yet not speaking too loudly of its price to be in keeping with the position and salary of the donor, and it was intended for Frances. After all, he acknowledged to himself, this was the gift in which he took the most pleasure, this was for the friend—the dearest—and he drew his breath quickly as he dared to say it to himself, and wondered what she would think if she knew he thought in this way about her. Then the eyes of the picture drew his irresistibly and, as he looked up, by some queer twist of memory, or hidden law of connection, there came to his mind the song that had been sung that evening:

> "I gave my life for thee,
> What hast thou given for me?"

and closely following upon the thought it brought came the verses he had learned from the Bible long ago:

"There is a Friend that sticketh closer than a brother." It came with startling clearness, as if it would remind him that there was a Friend whom he had forgotten, left out of his Christmas list after all, the very one for whom the Christmas festival was made in the beginning.

He sat down bewildered, and all the pretty prideful gifts he had arrayed stared back reproachfully at him. He sat ashamed before the pictured Christ.

In the sudden sense of shame that had come upon Gordon he looked away from the things he had bought so proudly but a few hours before, annoyed and unhappy, only to see what he had not noticed before, a chair on the other side of the room also piled high with packages. There was a large suit box, two of them in fact, and a hat box, with several paper parcels. They bore the advertisement of a firm of clothiers and men's furnishing goods on their covers.

The blood flamed high in the young man's face. He felt as if suddenly brought before a court of justice and convicted. These things were all for himself.

That great pile! And fifty cents in the collection basket the only thing he had shown as a Christmas gift to the Saviour of the world—his Saviour, for so in his heart he counted Christ.

He had a generous nature. He liked to give—when he had plenty to give from. He had never considered it so necessary to give very much toward religious institutions until to-night. Why was it that these thoughts were crowding out all the pleasure he was having in his purchases and the anticipated delight in giving them?

He turned impatiently and drew the chair full toward him with a jerk. He cut the strings viciously and unwrapped the parcels. Neckties! What did he want of more neckties? His bureau was simply swarming with them now in all the hues of the rainbow. But these were so pretty and so unusual! And just the colors Frances liked—and Frances had said those shades were becoming to him. Well, they were small things to scowl over. He tossed them gloomily aside.

Gloves! Yes, he must have new gloves to wear to the oratorio with Frances the night after Christmas. But he didn't need to buy two pairs just now. He could have waited for the others until after Christmas, and they would have been cheaper then, too.

The raincoat he had perjured his conscience to buy because it was a sample bargain and the last one of the lot, cut in a most unusual way, imported from one of London's great tailors, so the salesman had told him; that raincoat was disappointing now he looked at it with dull, critical eyes. It lay in a limp heap in the box with none of the crisp style to it that had charmed him when he saw it in the store and fancied himself swinging in its embrace down the Avenue holding an umbrella over Frances. He slid the box along on the carpet with the toe of his shoe, and opened the other box. He half hoped that the suit that he had had sent up would not fit. His old one would have done well enough for the oratorio of course, only this one had attracted him, and in the store he had felt quite virtuous to be buying a ready-made suit instead of one made to order, as Frances' brothers always did. Now it seemed even his virtue was an error. He sighed deeply and turned to the hat box for comfort.

To take Frances to the oratorio with this crown of well-dressed manhood upon his head was the fulfillment of a dream he had long dreamed. But now he took the hat from its box with little of the elation he had expected to feel. Somehow he did not like to look at the picture on the mantel and think of the souls without knowledge of Christ that he had heard about that evening, while he held that costly top-piece in his hand. After all, was a high hat so very desirable as he had thought? Was it as necessary to his earthly happiness as it had seemed but that afternoon?

He dropped the hat down in its box. He put the hat on his head viciously and glared at himself in the mirror, but the reflection did not do justice to his anticipation. He took it off and settled it on again, and looked at it critically, wondering if it was not a little too small, or maybe a little too large, and then threw it back ungently into the box and sat himself down to think.

He was unhappy! He felt that the only thing that could take this unhappiness away was to make it right with his conscience in some way. The only way to do that would be to give a goodly sum as a Christmas gift to that missionary or some other religious cause, he didn't care what. He felt mean, and that was the truth of the matter. He did not stop to tell himself that he had passed many Christmases before without a thought of giving a gift to Christ and been none the worse for it. Over and over until it came to be a din in his ears did that tenor voice ring,

> *"I gave my life for thee,*
> *What hast thou given for me?"*

He felt that he could not bear that reproach. Well, then, he must reconstruct his list. Perhaps he would have to change some of his presents for cheaper ones and get a little money in that way. He glanced up at the mantel instinctively. The little statue posed in its costly elegance. Not that! He could not change that. Frances headed his list. He could not make her present one whit less costly or beautiful, for she was dearest—here he paused. Was he setting Frances above his Lord? And could he hope to be blest in trying to win her love if he did so? This was not a thought of his own. He distinctly felt it was not. It was sent.

He looked hopelessly at the bright little things strewed about the bed. After all, was that giving a gift to take it out of his other friends? Had he any right to deprive them of their gifts? Ought it not to be a gift from himself rather than one cut off from what he had intended giving all his friends? And the gift to Christ should have come first in the planning. Christ should always stand first. Had he nothing he could give? Some sacrifice? Was there anything he had that he might sell, or—stay! There were the gold cuff buttons he bought last week. He had never worn them. They were three dollars and a half and were charged on father's bill. He could return them and have them credited, and that would be so much toward a gift to Christ. It would not seem as if the fifty cents stood so very much alone. But still, taken in contrast with the goodly gifts that lay about the room it was small and mean for the Christ of heaven—his Saviour.

Again the heap of clothing he had shoved aside called his attention. Those things were bought and paid for. He told them decidedly they could not be taken back. He was a stranger at that store. How would he look returning all those things? They would think he was crazy. But even as he thought this he remembered that the salesman had told him he could return the suit if it did not fit and the raincoat had been spoken of in the same way.

The salesman had said that if he did not like it on looking it over he could bring it back.

Then began a fight that lasted far into the night. Once or twice as he turned in his restless pacing to and fro he caught the face in the picture he had bought for his sister, and a fierce wish came over him to take that back where it came from. It had been the cause of all his trouble after all. But his better self knew this was folly, and the fight went on between himself and his selfishness.

At first it seemed to him that he was only giving room to an idle thought that troubled him and was trying to explain it all right to himself, but it did not explain. The more he thought about it the more there seemed to be something morally wrong about a professed Christian giving goodly gifts to those who needed them not, and buying fine raiment for himself and giving *nothing* to the Lord. The more this thought became clear to his mind, the more irritated he became, until suddenly facing his mirror, he saw his troubled, angry face full of petulant, childish self-will. Then, and behind it, reflected from the picture on the mantel, was the clear-eyed, boyish face of the pictured Christ, serene in the contemplation of matters of the Kingdom and His Father's business.

Himself in contrast with the Christ was something Gordon Pierce had never thought of before. He was startled. Not so much in the difference of the outward expression of his face and that of the picture, but in the character that both revealed.

He went back to his chair and dropped his face in his hands, and to his startled understanding there came a vision of the man he ought to be beside the man he was. For a little while the first question that had troubled him was lost sight of in the deeper thoughts that stirred his soul to their very depths. Even Frances was forgotten for the time while his soul met God and learned wherein he was found wanting.

A little while later he arose and reverently knelt beside his chair. It was the first thoughtful and unhurried prayer he had uttered since he was a little child and needed something very much of God.

"Oh, Christ!" he prayed. "I have not been worth much as a Christian. I've been thinking too much about my own pleasure. Forgive me, and help me to do better. I give myself to Thee as a Christmas gift to-night. It is a poor gift, but make it worth something for Thee."

When he got up from his knees he quietly and deliberately picked up the raincoat, the new suit, the neckties and the gloves and carefully folding them laid each in its individual box or paper as it had come. Over the hat he hesitated a moment, started to put it on again, and then abruptly put it in the box and tied the cover down. After that he went to bed.

In the brilliancy of the clear, cold morning that succeeded the night of storm, he started down-town an hour earlier than usual, his arms laden with many bundles. His fellow boarders eyed him curiously, for he did not usually burden himself with anything when he started out in the morning. He affected an elegant leisure in all his ways. This was not because of his upbringing, but because he had supposed it would beget him a dignity in keeping with one who aspired to friendship with one like Frances. But this morning he had forgotten all such thoughts; his set face showed determination and a will that would carry it out.

From counter to counter, from one department to another in the great store he went. He blessed the happy custom that made it possible for him to return these ill-advised purchases without wranglings and explanations.

When he reached the last place, however, and opened the box containing the beloved hat, the young salesman who had waited upon him happened to be sauntering near the exchange desk and recognized him. He raised his eyebrows slightly as he glanced significantly at the hat, and said enquiringly: "What's the matter? Didn't it fit?"

The blood flushed the customer's cheek and he felt as guilty as though he had stolen the hat. He answered unconcernedly: "I've decided to do without it." But he felt as though the whole miserable business was written in his face.

He was glad when his hands were empty and the money he had received in exchange for the various packages he had brought down-town was safely in his pocket. He counted it up mentally as he boarded the car that went toward his office, inwardly thankful that there was not much doing in his business this cold weather, and his presence at the office at an early hour was not so necessary as it would have been at another season of the year.

When he reached the office he found the general manager had been there and ordered some of the men off to another part of the city, and there would be nothing for him to do that morning. He sat at his desk for a little while doing some figuring and counting his money. At last with a happy face he counted out thirty dollars and rolled it together by itself. Then he took up the morning paper and turned to the notices of religious services held the night before. It took him some time to find the mention of the meeting he had attended, but at last he found it in an obscure corner. It gave him what he wanted, however, the name of the man who had spoken so eloquently about missions and the name of the pastor in whose church the meeting was held.

With a brighter face he donned his overcoat

and hat once more and hailing an up-town car was soon on his way to find the pastor. He was not at home, but his wife came to see the caller and explained that he would be away for a couple of days.

This was disappointment. When Gordon Pierce did anything he wanted to do it at once. Somehow those heathen in India would weigh on his soul and remind him of his lost high hat until the money he had decided to send them was out of his keeping. He drew his brows in perplexity. It had seemed so easy to hunt up this minister and ask him to send the money to the man who had spoken the evening before. The minister's wife studied the handsome young face before her and her heart went out in sympathy. She was used to helping young people when her husband was away through all sorts of trying times, from getting married to getting out of jail, so she asked a simple question sympathetically, and he opened his heart to her at once glad of a way out.

Her face brightened as she heard that it was money for the missionary.

"Oh, then, it will be all right!" she said eagerly. "Just take it to Mr. Adamson. He is the treasurer of our church and has charge of the money for Dr. Hanson's work. You will find him at his office on Chestnut Street. You know Adamson & Co. Just ask for Mr. Adamson, senior. I am so glad there is someone interested enough to take the trouble to bring some money. It was an interesting meeting last night, was it not? Too bad there were not more out, but then, it was wretched weather and so near to Christmas, too. People are selfish at Christmas in spite of everything. They will not come out or give. It was not a good time for a missionary meeting anyway, but we could not get Dr. Hanson any other time. Good-morning. I am glad you have called. I will tell my husband."

She bowed and smiled him out. He went down and gave his thirty dollars to the surprised Mr. Adamson, who looked with his keen business eyes at the young man glowing in the fervor of his first sacrifice for Christ, and wondered, but took the money and made a record of it with the name of the giver.

It was the night of the oratorio, and Gordon Pierce, with many a sigh, for the glow of sacrifice does not always last through the real part of the sacrifice itself, had arrayed himself in his old clothes, which were not so old except in comparison with new ones, and had donned his hat with many a thought of the hat that might have been, and gone after Miss

Frances. He had been invited to sit in their own private box with the family, and he knew it was a great honor. He always felt that when the sharp gaze of Frances' father rested upon him every defect of his life stood out in bold relief, and so he had been particularly anxious to appear as well as possible, for with Frances' father rested, after all, the final giving away of Frances herself to any young man, no matter how much he might love her or she love him.

And very nice indeed he looked as he sat beside her waving her unnecessary little fan just for sheer pleasure of doing something for her. Frances' father sat watching him critically and could not deny that he was handsome, but wished that he would not look so ardently into that beloved daughter's face. He had happened to pass through a store and had seen the young gentleman trying on a high hat, and Frances' father was a self-made man. He knew what high silk hats cost, and he happened to know the size of Gordon Pierce's salary. He could not forget that hat. He expected to have it in evidence very conspicuously this evening, but had been surprised to find that the young man did not wear it, and took pains to keep his hat out of sight. His observations at this point were interrupted by Mr. Adamson, his friend, who had seen him in the audience and at the intermission came over to the box to consult him about something important. The business finished, Mr. Adamson glanced up at the young man beside Frances.

"By the way," said he, "who is that young man?"

"That?" said the father, dejectedly brought back to the thorn that had been troubling him. "That is a young kid who thinks the universe centers around Frances. His name is Pierce. He is a civil engineer and doing well, but I'm afraid there isn't much in him."

"Well, he did strike me as that kind," said Mr. Adamson decidedly.

"Where did you meet him? What do you know of him?" asked Frances' father.

"He came to see me two or three days ago to give me some money for Dr. Hanson's mission. What did you say his salary was? I asked him if he was giving it himself, and he said, 'Yes.'"

"You don't say!" ejaculated Frances' father turning and regarding the flushed young man with a new interest. It was characteristic of Frances' father that he requested young Mr. Pierce to call at his office the next day.

"Young man,"—the millionaire knew how

to come directly to a point when he saw one, "where did you get that thirty dollars to give to missions?" he asked abruptly.

It seemed to Gordon that every folly and every tender feeling of his heart was to be stripped from him here and now, and he stood trembling as one condemned. He felt a sudden desire to cry as when a small boy he had seen the big boys run off with all the fun after he had helped work to get it. Then a rare quality of his came to the front, and he saw the funny side of the whole thing.

"From the fine clothes that I didn't buy," he answered with a choking laugh. "There was a high hat and an imported raincoat and a new suit and a lot of neckties."

"H'm!" said the old man regarding him severely, "and what did you want all those things for?"

"To appear well before your daughter, sir."

"Indeed! And why didn't you get them?" The face grew quizzical.

A glow came into Gordon's eyes.

"I did buy them," he answered quietly.

"What! Then how did you get the money back?"

"I bought them and had them sent home. Then I went to that meeting; the storm sent me in. It was not my own doing. I thought perhaps God sent me."

There was something grim in the older man's face. He had heard sentimentalists talk of God's doings in their lives before, and blame their own weaknesses on a higher power.

"I heard that man talk about those people who do not know about the Gospel. I heard some singing, too. I know you will not understand how I was stirred by it. Perhaps it will seem weak to you, but when I got home I got to thinking about it all, and looking over the things I had bought for myself and what I got for Christmas for my friends, father and mother and my sister—and the best I could afford for your daughter, for Frances, and something reminded me that I had given nothing to Christ. I can't explain to you, sir. It was only just that I felt that I had not been doing right by the Lord. I've never been any great Christian, but I never felt so mean in my life as I did that night. So the next morning I took all the things back that I had bought for myself and I figured up and found just how much money I could spare and get through the month, and I hunted up the man who talked and gave him the money. I don't see how you found out about it, sir."

There was quiet respect in Gordon Pierce's tones as he finished.

The old man wore a curious look of grim satisfaction.

"H'm!" he said at last, after calmly surveying his visitor.

"And might I presume to enquire why you wished to appear well before my daughter?"

"Because I love her."

The face of Frances' father softened about the grim mouth and keen eyes. He was remembering his own youth.

"And had you ceased to love her when you took back your fine clothes?"

"No," said he, "I loved her all the more, but I loved Christ best. I had bought your daughter's Christmas gift, but I had nothing for my Lord."

"Well," said the old man, turning toward his desk, "you did well. Perhaps you won't mind adding a little from me to that Christmas present you gave." He was writing in his check book now as if nothing had happened. The young man looked at him curiously and wondered how he should say what he must say before he left that office.

"There, I'll trouble you to hand that to Mr. Adamson from me to go with yours to missions. I don't mind encouraging a Christmas gift like that. I'll go without a high hat myself another year," and he chuckled dryly, and rubbed his hands together.

Gordon Pierce studied the check in his hands bewilderingly. It was filled out for three hundred dollars made payable to Mr. Adamson. His face brightened as he suddenly understood. He was glad beyond measure to have his gift recognized by one so much larger, and he felt the joy of the old man's approval. But there was something else he must ask before this interview ended.

He went over by the millionaire's desk and dared to grasp the hand that had held so many dollars. "Sir, I have told you that I love your daughter. I want to tell you that I am going to try to make her love me. Have I your permission to do so?"

The hands were clasped for a moment while the old eyes looked long into the young ones.

"Well, I guess you can do it, my boy. Go ahead."

Alone in his own room that night Gordon's first act was to kneel and thank his heavenly Father for the great gift of a woman's love that had been bestowed upon him. Then in glad resolve to make this new year a new life in every way he took down his neglected Bible and turning over the leaves, scarcely knowing how to begin a long broken habit, he lighted upon these words:

"Give and it shall be given to you—good measure, pressed down, shaken together and running over, shall men give into your bosom. For with the same measure you mete withal it shall be measured to you again."

Reverently he bowed his head as he realized that even then all gifts of his would never requite the great gift God had given to him that night.

The Story of the Lost Star

ABOUT a week before Christmas in a small city of the East there appeared in the Lost and Found column this advertisement:

> Lost. Sometime between the World War and the present morning, The Star of Bethlehem. The finder will confer everlasting favor and receive a reward of ten thousand dollars if returned to the owner between the hours of sundown and midnight on Christmas eve.
>
> (Signed) George K. Hamilton,
> Eleven, Harvard Place.

The type-setter blinked and paused in his busy work, read it again and wondered. Ten thousand dollars! Was it a joke? It must be a mistake! But no, it was paid for. It must go in.

He punched away at his machine and the lines appeared in the type, but his thoughts were busy. Ten thousand dollars! With that he could, with self respect, marry Mary! He would not have been John if he had not thought of that first.

George K. Hamilton. That was the rich guy who lived in the big house, with one blind wall stuck on its side that everybody said was a picture gallery. He was rolling in wealth so it must be real. But what was this thing he had lost that was worth everlasting favor and ten thousand dollars? A jewel? A silver tablet? Something of intrinsic historic value perhaps? Something that must be well known, or the writer would not have spoken of it in that off-hand indefinite way as *the* Star of Bethlehem, as if there were but one. Bethlehem—Bethlehem—that was the place where they made steel! Steel! Why—steel of course. George K. Hamilton. Hamilton the steel king! Ah! Why hadn't he thought of it at once?

And why couldn't he go to Bethlehem and find out all about it? He was the first one, excepting the editor of the Lost and Found column, to see this ad. Why wouldn't he stand first chance of the reward if he worked it right?

To be sure there was a possibility that some-one, who knew just what this star was, would be able to get on its track sooner, but if he caught the first train in the morning he would have a good start before anyone read the morning papers.

He would be through with his work by three a.m. at the latest, and there was a train at five. He would have time to get back to his boarding place and clean up a bit, perhaps scribble a note to Mary telling her to be ready for the wedding.

His fingers flew over the keys of his ma-chine as he laid his plans, and his heart throbbed with excitement over the great op-portunity that had flung its open door right in his humble path. Ten thousand dollars!

Early dawn saw him dressed in his best and hurrying on his way to Bethlehem amid a train load of laborers going out for the day's work. But he saw not pick nor shovel nor dinner pail, nor noted greasy overalls and sleepy-eyed com-panions. Before his shining eyes was a star, sometimes silver, sumptuously engraved, some-times gold and set in sparkling jewels, leading him on into the day of adventure.

He essayed to question his fellow seatmate about that star:

"You live in Bethlehem? Did you ever see the Star of Bethlehem?"

But the man shook his head dumbly:

"Me no spak L'angla!"

Arrived in the City of Steel he went straight to the news agent:

"Have you been here some time?"

"Born here."

"Then tell me, have you a Star of Bethlehem?"

The agent shook his head.

"Don't smoke that kind. Don't keep that kind. Try the little cigar store down the street." And he swung himself under the shelf and, shouldering a pile of morning papers, rushed off down the platform.

Out in the street John stopped a man whose foot was just mounting the running board of his car:

"Do you know anything about the Star of Bethlehem?"

"Never heard of it, Man. A Ford's good enough for me!" and he swung into his car and shot away from the curb hurriedly.

He asked a little girl who was hurrying away from the bakery with a basket of bread.

"Why, Star-of-Bethlehem is a flower," she said, "a little green and white starry flower with pointed petals. It grows in the meadow over there in the summer time, but it's all gone now. You can't find Stars-of-Bethlehem this time of year!" And she stared after him for a silly fool.

He asked a passer on the street:

"Can you tell me how to find out about Star of Bethlehem?"

The man tapped him lightly on the shoulder with a wink and advised him knowingly, with a thumb pointing down a side alley:

"You better not mention that openly, brother. There's been several raids around here lately and the police are wise. It ain't safe."

And about this time the Bishop back at home was opening the morning paper at the breakfast table as he toyed with his grapefruit and coffee:

"Ha, ha!" he said as his eye traveled down the column idly and paused at the Lost and Found, "Listen to this, Bella. Poor old George has got 'em again. He probably thinks he is going to die this time. I'll just step in and have a little talk on theology with him this morning and set his mind at rest. No need for that ten thousand dollars to go out of the church. We might as well have it at some home for the Feeble Minded."

Bella left her coffee and came around to read the advertisement, her face lighting intelligently:

"Oh, Basil! Do you think you can work it?" she cried delightedly.

"Why, sure, he's just a little daffy on religion now because he's been sick. The last time I saw him he asked me how we could know any of the creeds were true when they were all so different. I'll smooth it all out for him, and make him give another ten thousand or so to the Social Service work of our church, and he'll come across handsomely, you'll see. I'd better go at once. It won't do to wait, there are too many kinds of crooks on the lookout for just such a soft ten thousand as this." And he took his hat and coat and hurried out.

The Professor at his meagre breakfast table, worrying about his sick wife, and how he could afford to keep his eldest son in college, happened on the item.

He set down his coffee cup untasted and stepped to his book shelves taking down several wise treatises on Astronomy.

A sweet faced saint in an invalid chair read and pondered and murmured thoughtfully: "Poor soul! What's happened to the man's Bible?"

Before night the one little shop in the city that made a specialty of astronomical instruments had been drained of everything in the shape of a searcher of the heavens, and a rush order had gone on to New York by telegraph for more telescopes of various sizes and prices, while a boy in the back office who was good at lettering was busy making a copy of the advertisement to fasten up in the plate glass window, with special electric lights playing about it and a note below:

"Come in and order your telescope now before they are all gone, and get into line for the great sky prize! We have 'em! All prices!"

Far into the evening the crowd continued around that window and many who had glasses at home hurried away to search for them, and build air castles of how they would spend the ten thousand dollars when they got it.

Even before the day was half over the office of the University was besieged by eager visitors come to question wise ones, a folded newspaper furtively held under each applicant's arm.

As evening drew on shadowy figures stole forth to high places and might have been seen scanning the heavens, and now and then consulting a book by means of a pocket flash light.

More than one young student worked into the small hours of the night with reference books scattered about him, writing a many-paged treatise on the Star of Stars, some to prove that the star was a myth, and others that it was still in existence and would one day appear again as bright as of old. Even the police, coming suddenly upon lurking star-gazers far toward morning, began to question what had taken hold of the town.

Coming home on the late train from a fruitless search for an unknown quantity which was not there, John Powers sat wearily back in the fusty seat of the common car and took out the worn advertisement from his pocket to read it once more.

The lost Star of Bethlehem! What could it be? He had searched the steel city from end to end without finding so much as a trace of tradition or story about a star in connection with that town. He had met with more rebuffs and strange suggestions than ever before in his life together, and he was dog-weary and utterly discouraged. If only he had not written that hopeful letter to Mary in the morning!

Now perhaps she would already be planning to have the wedding soon, and where was the money coming from to provide the little home?

Of course it just might happen that after all the star had been lost up in the city, else why should the advertisement have been put in the city paper and not in the Bethlehem local? But even so he had hoped great things from this trip to Bethlehem and now he had only wasted a day and the car fare, and had gotten nowhere at all.

At a local station a loud mouthed traveler got off, leaving his recent seatmate without anyone to talk to, and presently he joined John Powers and entered into conversation, being one of those men who is never happy unless his tongue is wagging. In the course of their talk, John found himself asking the old question again:

"You say you are from Bethlehem? Did you ever hear of a star in connection with that town? Was there any memorial tablet or monument or emblem or anything in the shape of a star, that has been stolen away? Star of Bethlehem it was called, do you know anything about it?"

The stranger stared blankly and shook his head:

"Sounds to me as if it might be a song, or a book mebbe. If you knowed who wrote it you might find out at one o' the schools. My

Johnny says you can find out almost anything if you know who wrote it. Ever been a Mason? Might be some kind of a Masonic badge, mightn't it?"

The man got out at the next station and Powers leaned back wearily and thought how he had failed. His mind seemed too tired to think any longer on the subject.

An old lady in a queer bonnet with many bundles at her feet and a basket beside her out of which stuck a pair of turkey's feet, leaned over suddenly and touched him on the shoulder:

"Laddie, hae ye tried the auld Buik?" she asked timidly, "I'm thinkin' ye'll find it all there."

"I beg your pardon!" said Powers lifting his hat courteously and thinking how the blue of her eyes had a light like that in Mary's eyes.

He arose from his seat and went back to sit beside her. Then somehow the blue of her eyes made him unafraid, and he told her all about the ten thousand dollars and his fruitless trip to Bethlehem.

"Oh, but laddie, ye're on the wrong track entirely," said the old lady. "The Star o' Bethlehem's in the auld Buik. I ken it's no the fashion to read it these days, but the worruld lost sight of a lot besides the things it wanted to forget when it set out to put its Bibles awa! Hunt up yer Mither's Bible, lad, and study it out. The star arose in the East ye ken, and the folks who saw it first was those that was lookin' fer its arisin'. The star's *na* lost. It led to the little King ye ken, an' it'll always lead to the King if a body seeks with all the heirt, fer that is the promise: 'An' ye shall find me, when ye shall seek fer me with all yer heirts.' May like the puir buddy who wrote the bit lines in the paper was longin' fer the King hisself an' wanted the star to guide him, but ye ken ye can't purchase the gifts of God wi' silver ner gold. The mon may lay his ten thousand baubles at the fut of the throne, but he'll find he must go his own self across the desert, and wait mayhap, before he'll ever see the shining' of the Star. But you'll not turn back yerself now you've started, laddie! Go find the King fer yerself. Look in the Gospels an' read the story. It's passin' wonderful an' lovely. This is my station now, and I'll be leavin' ye, but it'll be a glad Christmas time fer you ef you find the little King, an *ye'll find Him* sure, if ye seek on with all yer heirt."

The doorway to the fine old Hamilton mansion on Harvard Place was besieged from morning to night all that week by aspirants wishing to speak with the Master, but to all the grave and dignified servitor who answered the door replied:

"My master is away. He cannot speak with you until the time appointed. If any then have found the lost treasure they may come and claim the reward. But they must come bringing it with them. None others need present themselves."

Even the Bishop had not been able to gain admittance. He was much annoyed about it. He was afraid others would get ahead of him. He had written a letter, but he knew it had not yet been opened for the last time he called he had seen it lying on the console in the hall with a lot of other unopened letters. The Bishop was very certain that if he could have audience *first* all would be well. He was sure he could explain the philosophy of life and the mystery of the star quite satisfactorily and soothingly.

Before John Powers had gone back to work that night of his return from Bethlehem, he had gone to the bottom of an old chest and hunted out his mother's Bible. It was worn and dropping apart in places, but he put it tenderly on his bed, and following an impulse, dropped to his knees beside it, laying his lips against its dusty covers. Somehow the very look of the old worn covers brought back his childhood days and a sense of sin in that he had wandered so far from the path in which his mother had set his young feet.

All that week he gave all the extra time he had to studying about the star. He did not even go to see Mary. He lost sight of the ten thousand dollars in his interest in the star itself. He was now seeking to find that star for himself, not for the reward that had been offered. He wanted to find the King who was also a Saviour.

The last night before it came time for him to go to his work, he dropped upon his knees once more beside the little tattered book, and prayed:

"Oh, Jesus Christ, Saviour of the world, I thank Thee that Thou hast sent Thy star to guide me to Thee. I worship Thee, and I give myself to Thee forever."

* * *

On Christmas eve when the door of the mansion was thrown open a large throng of people entered, and were speedily admitted, one by one, to audience with the master of the house, until, in an incredibly short space of time, the waiting room was emptied of philosophers and dreamers and ambitious ones. Even the Bishop had been courteously sent his way. Only three were left. Three wise ones, and two of them were women!

One was an old woman with a burr upon her tongue and a Bible in her hand; one was a young girl with blue starry eyes and a bit of a Testament in the folds of her gown where she kept her fingers between the leaves to a place. The third was John Powers, standing within the shadow of a heavy curtain beside a deep-set window looking out at the great shining of a bright star, with peace upon his face. He turned about as the door closed after the Bishop and glanced at the two women. The girl looked up and their eyes met.

"Mary!"

"John!"

There was scarcely time to recognize the old woman before the door opened and George K. Hamilton, keen of eye, sharp of feature, eager of expression, walked in and looked from one to the other searching each face questioningly.

The young man stepped forward to meet him and Mary saw for the first time that a worn little Bible was in his hand.

But John was speaking in such a ringing voice of certainty:

"Sir, I want to tell you first that I have not come for your money. When I began this search it was in hope of the reward, but I've found the Star itself, and it led me to the King, and now I've brought it to you because I want you to have it too. You'll find it in this Book. It has to be searched for, but it's there. And when you have found it I've been thinking you'll maybe want to sell all that you have and give to the poor and go and follow *Him*. But *I* am not one of those poor any longer, for I *have found the King!* Come, Mary, shall we go?"

Then up rose the old Scotch woman from her place near the door:

"I've just one more word to say, an' ye'll find it in yon Buik: 'Arise, shine; for thy light is come, and the Glory of the Lord is risen upon thee.' That star isn't lost, sir, an' never was! Never will be! It's up in the heavens waiting till the King has need of it again, and some day it will burst upon the world again and they will all know that it has been there all the time!"

The Master was left alone in his mansion with the book in his hand and a strange awed feeling of the Presence of God in his room.

He looked wonderingly, doubtfully, down at the book, and then wistfully out through his richly draped window to where a single star shone softly through the Christmas night.

The Handmaid of the Lord

IT was long past midnight and the city of Jerusalem was sleeping. Even the far dim stars seemed to have withdrawn, and a great silence was abroad, as if the earth were waiting for some momentous catastrophe that was to break on the morrow.

Down a narrow dark street in the more crowded portion of the city a stealthy figure walked, drawing his rough coat about him and shivering as he stole along, watching each cross street furtively either way and skulking out of sight into a doorway whenever other pedestrians appeared. He was startled even at a gaunt dog that stalked across his pathway; he drew out of sight until the dog was gone.

Halfway down the street he paused before a plain insignificant house tucked between two larger ones. Slipping close, he stood a moment listening, cautiously peering around the corner of an arched doorway into a paved passage between the houses, and then gave three taps twice repeated upon the door. Though they were cautiously given, yet they re-echoed throughout the narrow street, and the visitor withdrew into the covered passage and kept watch until he heard one coming to open the door.

Presently a crack of light appeared beneath the door, and a glimmer in the lattice above. A low voice demanded who was there.

For answer, the visitor tapped rhythmically with the tips of his fingers a bit of code that seemed to be understood, for the door was opened a crack, and a woman's voice asked once more, "Who is it?"

"Is Mary, the wife of Joseph, staying here?" asked the stranger sidling closer to the door.

"She is resting now," explained the woman in a guarded tone. "She has had a hard evening. I have persuaded her to try to sleep. Perhaps in the morning she can see you."

"I must see her at once," demanded the stranger gruffly. "It is important!" and he slid a foot within the crack of the door and looked furtively behind him up and down the dark street.

"Is it—about—?" the woman lowered her voice to a whisper.

"Yes!" said the man. "About her Son. Jesus! Won't you call her?"

"Oh! has something more happened?" The woman's hand went to her heart.

"Plenty!" said the man harshly. "Let me come in. It is not well that I should be seen here. I must speak with Mary at once. Make haste for the time is short!"

He pushed roughly inside the door and made it fast behind him.

"Who?" asked the woman peering into the dark face by the light of the tiny lamp which she held high, whose wick was almost spent. "Who shall I say is come?"

"No matter!" said the man turning his face into the shadow. "Tell her it is one of His friends."

"I do not think I have met you," the woman hesitated. "I have been with her all the evening."

"Won't you make haste?" snapped the man roughly. "It matters not who I am. I bring her important news. I must see her at once! If you will not call her, I shall search the house for her. I have no time to trifle."

With a frightened glance back of her, the

woman turned and hurried into an inner room, leaving the lamp blinking upon the table beside the man, who stood impatiently tapping his sandaled foot on the earthen floor.

There was a sound of low voices, a frightened exclamation, and then hurried steps in the next room. The door was opened, and Mary stood in the room, a look of fear on her delicate, exquisite features. Her hands were clasped convulsively over her heart as if with terrible premonition, traces of recent tears were upon her pale cheeks, her eyes were large with anxiety as she peered into the shadows of the room to see the man who stood lowering beside the door. Then she stepped nearer and lifted the lamp to throw the light more freely on his features.

Suddenly she put down the lamp upon the table, her face hardened into scorn and indignation.

"You?" she exclaimed in a low, challenging voice. *"You! Judas!* You *dared* to come to me?"

The man cringed angrily into the shadow and put up a hand to stay her speech.

"Listen!" he said gruffly, "I have words to speak to you!"

"And why should I listen to you?" asked Mary in a clear tone that could be heard distinctly by her friend at the door of the inner room. "If there were some news of Him, could they not have sent a *friend* and not an enemy? If He is dead, Judas, *you* have killed Him! You, who pretended to be one of His most earnest followers! I know what you have done! I have heard it all from an eye-witness!"

"He is not dead," said Judas sullenly, "and I have done nothing but what should have been done. What I did, I did for His sake!"

"For *His* sake!" said Mary contemptuously. "You betrayed Him with a *kiss!*" Her voice was hot with scorn.

"I did it for His sake!" persisted Judas. "The time had come when, if He was to be placed upon the throne, He must be made to manifest His power and show what He was and what He could do. Just little miracles were not enough any more. There must be some great public manifestation. I was sure that when He saw that He was hopelessly in the hands of His enemies, with soldiers surrounding Him, He would be forced to manifest His power and show them that He was what He claimed to be. If He had passed through their midst and disappeared, got out of their hands miraculously, there are many who would have believed on Him at once. It would have been nothing then to have gathered an army and put Him immediately upon the throne. But now—!"

"But now?" repeated Mary, her eyes bright with scorn, her lips thin with anguish and indignation.

"Well, now He simply left us in the lurch!"

"Left *you* in the lurch? What do you mean?"

"Why, you understand of course," answered the man, "that if we put Him on the throne we naturally expected some pretty good offices in the new Kingdom. But He seems to have forgotten all about that, just left us in the lurch!—failed us miserably. He has let Himself be drawn into a terrible strait. He simply played into their hands. I can only think He had been asleep and did not realize—or—perhaps He is figuring even yet to perform some greater miracle, break the bands that bind Him, and show the world what He is; but He has gone too far! He does not seem to realize what power the Sanhedrin has. He simply lost His nerve and went with them as quietly as if it were nothing, without a word of protest! He thinks, I suppose, that He will be able to argue them out of it with wise words. But things have gone too far for that. It is too late for that sort of thing. Something must be done at once or there is no hope left. They have taken Him to Pilate! And Pilate dare not be friendly! He has too much to lose!"

"To Pilate!"

Mary stepped back with a quick convulsive pressure of her hand upon her heart, new anguish in her eyes, and reeled as if she would have fallen, had not her friend Salome stepped from the doorway and put a steadying arm about her.

Then Mary rallied and her eyes flashed fire.

"They have taken Him to Pilate! My Son! My Holy One! And you stand here, you who are responsible for it, to prate and excuse yourself and say you did it for His sake! Stand aside! Don't waste my time further! I must go to Him!"

"That is what I have come here for, to take you to Him," answered the man. "But first, I must tell you something. There is something you can do, a way to save Him if you will."

Mary turned upon him quickly.

"What do you mean, something *I* can do? When *you* have done your worst? And who are *you* to tell *me* how to save Him? Am I to pay you thirty more pieces of silver to have you use your tainted influence to save Him after you have sold Him for your own gain?

You traitor! You who sold your Lord for silver! Would you also ask more silver of me, His anguished mother?"

"You do not trust me!" whined the man. "I swear I come as a friend, yet you do not trust me!"

"No! I do not trust you! Can one trust a traitor?"

"You will not feel so when I have told you what I have come to suggest," answered the man suavely. "Listen! The time grows short. Even now Pilate may be on the point of ordering the soldiers to bring Him forth for trial. The morning is about to dawn. Because of the feast, they will hurry this business through. He will be tried perhaps at daybreak—early, they said, and I hurried straightway to tell you. For, Mary, mother of Jesus, you, *you* are the *only* one who can save Him now! He might have saved Himself if He had chosen, but now He has shown that He cannot save Himself. There must be found another way. And I have found it. There is still hope for Him if you will do one thing. Would you let your Son go to His death because you would not listen?"

Mary caught her breath in a quick agonized sob, her eyes aflame with anguish, as she watched her tormentor.

"Oh! *You!*" she cried desperately. "You goad me with your words till I cannot refuse, though I feel in my heart you are His enemy! Well, say on! What have you to propose? I will not have it said that I blindly refused. Speak quickly! What is there that I can do?"

"Sit down!" said the man trying to put a gentler note into his cold voice, "you are worn and weary and can listen better so!"

"I *stand!*" said Mary firmly.

"All right. Have it your own way. Well, then, it is this. You know that the whole trouble centers about His assertion of deity. If that were denied, the matter would be dropped, and the Jews would be appeased. He is arrested because He claims to come from God, to be the expected Messiah. Take that claim from Him, and it would be as easy to get Him released as any common criminal, like Barabbas, for instance."

A long shiver of horror went through Mary as he spoke, but she controlled herself and flashed him a quick scornful look.

"And what has that to do with me?" she asked.

"Everything!" he answered with a kind of satisfaction in his voice. "Because it happens that you are the only one who can take that from Him. This tradition of holiness with which you have surrounded Him, the hint that He is not Joseph's child, makes all the difference in the world. You have only to deny that He is of heavenly parentage, and the trouble will all drop away. And then it will be easy, when He is released, to spirit Him away into the hills for a time, for rest and recuperation from a nervous breakdown, you know, until all be forgotten. Then we can prepare an army secretly, when the trouble has quieted down and the Sanhedrin is not expecting it, to put Him upon the throne, and all will yet be well."

"You mean—?" asked the mother with slow, awe-stricken utterance, and white, horrified lips.

"I mean," went on the assured voice of the man, "that you are to come forward as His mother and say that He is really Joseph's child after the flesh; that all this talk about His being the Messiah is a mistake; that you never meant people to understand that He was of miraculous birth. People will believe you. You are well respected here. And you are the only one in the whole world who rightly knows His parentage. If you are unwilling to have Joseph stand as His natural father, then say who *is* His father. A little blight upon your honor will not matter to you, I know, against the possibility of His death. And when He sits upon the throne, it will not matter that you have borne dishonor for a few days."

Mary was white to the lips. She stood back now with clenched hands down at her sides, the full light of the flickering, spent little wick flaring upon her face and lighting it with a glow of righteous wrath.

"You mean," and she caught her breath to make her voice more clear, "you mean that I should *lie* to save my Holy One from death? You mean that I should make *His own* words *lies?*"

"If it *is* a lie," sneered the man shrugging his shoulders. "Yes, a little lie like that to save a life! It is nothing!"

"It is *everything!*" proclaimed Mary, her voice suddenly rising in a kind of exultant throb. "It is His very life and being, the purpose for which He was sent into the world! It would mean discrediting the word of angels, and the message from God Himself. It would mean denying the power of the Most High! Destroy His heavenly parentage, and you destroy the Saviour of the world—and make Him a liar and a criminal—or crazy!"

"Call it crazy then!" laughed the man. "I—have sometimes—wondered—if—He wasn't!"

"Ah!" said Mary looking at him piercingly, "and yet they said that you believed on Him! Well, listen, now, you traitor! You have said that I was the only one who knew the truth about His heavenly origin. Yes, that is true. It was to me the angel came and told me what high honor Heaven was sending to me, a humble maiden. I have kept all His words in my heart. It is I who know how the power of the Most High came upon me. It is I who have pondered these great things all His wonderful life, and watched to see my Jesus grow up for His great mission. Yes, I know! And *never* will I soil my Holy One by denying the truth about Him! God knows that I would give this heart of mine and let it be torn asunder and laid bare to the world to set Him free from His enemies. But never will I dishonor my God by telling cheap lies to save my Son for any man-planned kingdom. If God wills that He should go to His death that He may fulfill His plan for Him, so be it, but I will never deny the truth! Go, Judas, self-steeped soul, enemy of Jesus the Son of God! Traitor! *Satan!* Thinking to outwit God! *Go!* No word of mine shall ever deny the holy power of the Most High, nor thus undo the mischief that your traitor kiss has wrought!"

Mary turned her back upon him and walked from the room, closing the door with finality. Judas, darkly frowning, baffled, slid from the door and was gone into the night; and the morning of that saddest day of all the world crept softly into the sky, like one who knew its brightness was soon to be darkened by the sin of the world.

Then Salome crept softly to the door of her guest's room and quietly knelt beside her as she wept upon her bed.

"Mary, dear," she whispered with a sympathetic arm about her friend, "I couldn't help hearing what he said. Of course I feel the same way you do about Judas. I never did like him. And I can understand that you were angry; but—wasn't there reason this time in what he said? It is true, isn't it, that the charge they have made against Him is that He claims to be the King of the Jews, the long expected Messiah, the Holy One that is to come, born miraculously? And wasn't Judas right in saying that if that could be denied, He might be set free? Mary, at a time of stress like this, and for so good a cause, surely there would be no harm in your saying that it is not true—that Joseph—or somebody else—*was* His father. What harm could there be in that? Why won't you do it, dear?"

"Because it is not *true!*" said Mary lifting her tear-stained face to look earnestly at her friend in the dim light of the dawn. "Because it is according to the angel's message, and God's Word, that He was of heavenly origin. Because I *know* what I know! I would be most unworthy of my wonderful Son if I were to deny His heavenly Fatherhood!"

"But Mary, not to *save* His life?"

"Not to save His life, Salome! He would not want it, my friend. You do not know Him if you think He would."

Then suddenly upon the outer door came insistent knocking and a sound of voices talking.

Hastily Salome rose and went to answer the knock.

"It is your other sons, Mary!" she whispered, coming back. "They want to see you at once. Don't look so frightened, dear; nothing has happened. The Sanhedrin has not yet come together."

Then Mary went again to the outer room and stood among her stalwart sons.

"Mother, we have come to see you about

Jesus," spoke the eldest of them. "He has got Himself into real trouble at last, just as we told you He would if a stop wasn't put to His nonsense. He is to be tried quite early this morning, in an hour perhaps, and according to all we can find out about it, the odds are entirely against Him. The Sanhedrin is disgusted with all the excitement and wild talk of miracles. That business about Lazarus being raised from the dead has put the finishing touch to it. And now there is no hope for Him, unless—well, Mother, we've thought of a way. At least a way has been suggested."

She gave him a quick bright look, with hope dawning in her eyes. Was there a way to save Him? Yet these brothers of His were not in sympathy with Him, she remembered with a sharp pang. Would it be a *possible* way? They had always disparaged His ministry, disagreed with His way of life, and called it visionary. They had driven Him from His home.

Then out spoke the youngest brother eagerly. He had never been quite so hard as the rest, had always tried to smooth the way between them all, to placate and explain.

"Mother, don't look so worried. It's practically an easy thing to get Him off if you will only agree. Just a few words from you, and everything will be all right. I know it may be a bit embarrassing to you, but you won't mind, I'm sure, if this thing can only be hushed up and Jesus set free. Our family has never been mixed up in publicity this way, and we don't want to begin now. It's nothing much, Mother, it's just that claim that He is virgin born that is making all the trouble. If you will only be willing to say it wasn't so—it could be done in a few words and quite quietly, to a few who have influence—it could all be hushed up and Jesus released. Everyone would understand and respect you, Mother. All you would need to do would be to tell them that our father was of course Jesus' father too. And I'm sure that Father, if he were here, would quite approve. He was always so reasonable, and always treated Jesus just like one of us. Come, Mother, get your things on. There isn't much time to spare!"

Suddenly Mary clasped her hands and looked up, drawing a deep breath.

"Oh, if my Joseph were only here!" she cried. "He knew all about it. He would understand. God spoke to him in a dream and told him that my Jesus was from on high, and Joseph believed it. Oh, your father would understand, my son, yes he would understand,

and he and I could never deny what God has done. My Jesus *is* the *very Son of God!*"

Out into the morning at last went the stalwart sons, unable to move their frail little mother, marvelling at her strength, and stubbornness, as they called it, over such a small matter that meant so much to the family pride just now. They walked along the waking streets where smug Sanhedrin members took an eager way to Pilate's Hall, rubbing their hands in satisfaction as they met one another with gravely congratulatory bows. The prey was in their hands at last. The troublesome One would soon be dealt with, and the people return to reasonableness and ritual and formality.

And Mary, as she waited for her friend to make ready, knelt alone beside the bed whereon she had not slept that night, and let her heart stand still before her God, yielding her will to His, feeling the consciousness that He was still using her, going over in her heart all the words of the angel Gabriel. Ah! It did not look this morning as if all nations could call her blessed, as the world counts blessedness! Mother of a Son about to be tried for His life!

And a word from her, a little *lie,* could set

him free! And perhaps undo the plan of the eternal God for the ages to come! But the God of gods had promised! He knew the end from the beginning! There was nothing to do but trust Him! In her sorrowing soul she bowed and said softly to Him once more:

"Behold the handmaid of the Lord; be it unto me according to Thy word," and she knew within herself that her precious privilege of suffering for her wonderful Son was not yet over.

Then she remembered the words of her cousin Elizabeth, long ago, especially those last few words: "Blessed is she that believed: for there shall be a performance of those things which were told her of the Lord."

And God had performed it all as He had told her, could she not trust the future of that Son with Him who had sent Him, as well as she had trusted His past?

Then suddenly with a stab of pain came the memory of old Simeon's words to her: "Yea, a sword shall pierce through thy own soul also." Was this what those words had meant? Her soul shrank within her in apprehension. And yet there was nothing she could do but trust, and if God could work His will through a crucified Jesus, who was she to try to prevent it by denying the great miraculous truth, and setting a lie ringing down the ages?

So Mary arose and went forth to Calvary.

Now on the way they passed the praetorium. A great crowd was assembled there, and as Mary and Salome skirted about it, they saw Mary's other sons.

The youngest one came and took her arm.

"What is it all about?" she asked fearfully as the crowd jostled her back against the wall.

Her son drew her up into a doorway where she could see over the heads of the people, and as they looked, there on the great stone platform of the place called The Pavement, came forth Pilate, and One after Him clad in a purple robe with a crown of cruel thorns upon His head.

"There! You see, Mother," whispered her son, "they are mocking Him. That is my brother! Think of it, *my brother,* up before the eyes of the common herd! And *you* might have saved us all this by just a few words. But listen! Pilate is speaking now. Hark, I want to hear what he says!"

Pilate's voice was clear, and the mob was suddenly hushed as he spoke. Mary heard the words quite distinctly:

"I bring Him forth to you, that ye may

know that I find no fault in Him! Behold, the man!"

Mary caught her breath, and a great wave of hope rushed over her. If Pilate found no fault, why, surely He might be saved!

But suddenly from all about her there arose a cruel snarl of cries: "Crucify Him! Crucify Him!" Some of those voices, too, came from chief priests and officers. But Pilate's voice was ringing out again:

"Take *ye* Him and crucify Him: for *I* find no fault in Him."

Then up rose a cruel-faced man, wearing pompous robes, and claimed attention, speaking to Pilate, and hushing the mob into silence.

"We have a law," he said ominously, "and by our law He ought to die, because He made Himself *the Son of God!*"

Mary drew in her breath sharply.

"There it is, Mother, just as we told you!" her son whispered in her ear. "It is for that absurd claim they are killing Him, nothing else. And one word from you would set it all right. Do it now, Mother, while there is yet time! Do it now, and let us slip Him away out of sight quickly before the mob is roused again. I'll lead you up to Pilate. See, there is a way behind that group of men! Pilate does not want to crucify Him. He will listen to you if you will go."

But Mary's eyes were on her Son, that precious heavenly face with a glory in the eyes that other faces seemed not to know. Those cruel thorns pressed into His loved brow, that brow she had kissed and fondled when He was a little babe! How her heart was wrung to see Him so, mocked at and scorned, the great men of the council wishing to kill Him! Her Holy One! That purple robe! With what dignity He wore it! And even a thorny crown, how royally it sat upon His brow! Why could they not see it, those chief priests and scribes who called themselves wise; why could they not realize with what royal bearing He wore the robes put upon Him in scorn?

Ah! She could not stand it to see Him so! Almost she yielded to her son's urgency. Almost! But then Pilate spoke again. He was not speaking to the crowd now. He was looking straight at Jesus. But she could hear every word. "Whence art thou?"

Mary looked eagerly toward her Son. Now she would have the word from His own lips. But no! He was not speaking at all! What could it mean?

"There! Mother!" sneered the younger brother with contempt in his voice. "There's your miracle-worker! He hasn't the nerve to answer! He can't stand up for Himself! *My brother!*"

But Pilate was speaking again:

"Speakest thou not unto me? Knowest thou not that I have power to crucify thee, and have power to release thee?"

Ah! Now He was answering at last.

"Thou couldst have no power at all against Me except it were given thee from above."

Mary drew back and pulled away from the urgency of the young arm that would have drawn her toward the stone seat of judgment where Pilate sat. No, that was her answer. It was not for her to deny God's wonders. "Thou couldst have no power at all against Me except it were given thee from above." That was her reminder that she was the handmaid of the Lord, that somehow this thing was of Him.

And then the crowd surged in. They were leading Him away. Her Jesus! Her precious baby!

She thought of Him in the manger smiling so sweetly from the straw. She remembered the wonderful star that had blazed forth over the stable where he lay. She thought of the shepherds who came to worship and their tale of angel-messages: Peace on earth! And He was being led away to be crucified! She thought of the wise men and their strange symbolic presents! She remembered prophecies about Him which she had not understood!

And now they were making him bear His cross!

She caught one glimpse of Him through her tears as He sank under it. She remembered the promise of the angel that He was to be great and that God was to give Him the throne of his father David! And now He was lying on the pavement beneath a cross, a crown of thorns upon His head! The Son of God! She was not hearing her other son's words as he tried to lead her home away from it all, telling her that it was too late now. But though the words came with a thud against her soul she knew that even if it had not been too late she could not have denied His heavenly origin.

Calvary at last, and the awful sound of the hammers driving nails! Nails through the precious hands! Oh those rosy baby hands! She had so often laid reverent lips to kiss their palms! She sank with the other women on a hillock and covered her face, hearing those awful hammer blows! Her Jesus! Her precious Jesus! *Her Lord!*

Oh, could mortal mother bear these sounds and not cry out, *even a lie* to save Him? She rose and staggered up the hill. Her Babe of Bethlehem! Her sweet little Babe with His heavenly smile! Oh, if she might but just have permission from God to deny His origin and save Him yet!

She saw the insults that followed, she saw them spit into His precious face, and jeer. She saw them slap Him in the face with the backs of their gnarled hands, she saw them bartering His garments that she had wrought with such loving care. She heard them call upon Him to save Himself, to show His kingship!

She saw the blood drops falling down His brow from the cruel thorns! Oh could mortal mother endure that sight and not do something? *Anything!* Perhaps it was not too late even yet! Perhaps Pilate was up there near the cross and she could go and tell him that it was all an awful mistake!

But it was not a mistake! And she knew in her heart that even though she should lie to shield Him, He would claim His heavenly origin to the end! He *wanted* her to do the same.

She staggered to her feet and went nearer, dropping down at the very foot of the cross looking up, and He looked down and caught her glance! Through all His anguish, He yet had thoughts for her, and wanted her to understand that *He* knew what she was passing through, and that He was pleased, satisfied with her loyalty.

And then He spoke! Oh, wonder of wonders! He called John and gave her into his care! Ah! How precious! The tears flowed down without their former bitterness!

"But O, God in heaven! Will You let Your Son die without a sign? Though You carry out Your purpose for the ages through a crucified Jesus, will You not at least give some sign to the world that He is the Son of God?"

Suddenly Mary realized that though it was high noon darkness was coming down over the earth! Heaven itself was putting out its light to condemn the awful deed, and testify to the truth of the claim of the Holy One!

It was then the earthquake came! Strange quiverings of the ground, awful rending of rocks, and rumblings! Ah, God was showing the earth its awful sin!

Suddenly, beside her some one spoke. It was a voice she did not know, perhaps a centurion standing by the cross, but the words were spoken with profound earnestness and conviction:

"Truly, this was the Son of God!"

Mary heard, and lifted her bowed head. Oh! Suppose she had told a lie to save *Him?* She was glad, *glad* that she had remained firm to the end. This one man at least had been convinced of the truth even through her son's death, and there would be others! She lifted trusting eyes to heaven.

Then down at her feet, the lie, which had lain coiled like a serpent, looking at her with great evil green eyes, ready for her use should she weaken, slowly uncoiled and slunk away— not to die, only to lie coiled and hidden, awaiting other times, when other souls less faithful through other years, should find it and bring it forth, to dishonor the eternal Son of God with blasphemies, and to deceive "them that perish; because they received not the *love of the truth* that they might be saved. . . . God shall send them strong delusion that they should believe a lie! that they all might be damned who believed not the truth but had pleasure in unrighteousness."

The Best Birthday

Foreword

DOWN Fairview Road in Swarthmore, Pa., there is a lovely little old stone church surrounded by a quaint cemetery. It is known as the Old Leiper Church, and has a Sunday School in which I have been working for a good many years.

One Christmas we decided that in place of the usual common-place Christmas tree, and the usual "pieces" recited and sung in honor of Christmas, it would be well to have something that would fix in all our minds the real meaning of Christmas, making plain the prophecies concerning Christ's coming and their fulfillment, and making God's plan of salvation the central thought.

So I chose two young boys to be the leading characters, boys old enough to understand what we were trying to do, young enough to enter into the spirit of the "play," as they called it, earnest enough to care about it and work faithfully, gifted enough to speak clearly and distinctly, so that they would gain the instant attention and interest of the audience. Then I called in all the rest of the girls and boys who were willing to help us, and we began to build this program.

For it was not all written at one sitting. It grew as we began to practise it, and as other girls and boys came into it. The average age of the participants was from twelve to fifteen years, though there were some as young as seven who had small parts, and some as old as seventeen.

All of them were interested, and all of them realized that there might be some in their audience who did not know the Lord Jesus who came to die for their sins, or some who had been taught to doubt whether the story of salvation was true, and that it might be in God's plan to use this simple setting forth of proofs to convince some heart and lead some-one to accept the Lord Jesus Christ as his personal Saviour.

So, for three successive Christmases we have given this story of "The Best Birthday" over again, with the same young actors taking the parts. The actual given names of our young people are used in the text.

And because others have heard about it, and asked to have the program printed, I am putting it into practical form. And we, the young people and I who have been giving it, send greetings and glad Christmas wishes to all who shall care to use it hereafter.

GRACE LIVINGSTON HILL

A GROUP of young people, headed by JOE march up the left aisle, joyously singing the first verse of number 2, PINEBROOK CHORUSES, "Oh, Say But I'm Glad!"

CHARLIE, walking slowly up the right aisle, watches them wistfully, and meets them just in front of the pulpit as the singing ends.

CHARLIE
Say, what makes you kids look so happy? Your faces are just on a broad grin.

JOE
We are happy! Christmas is coming!

ALL (except Charlie)
Yes! Christmas! *Merry* Christmas!

CHARLIE
Oh, Christmas! What's Christmas? I suppose

you kids are going to hang up your stockings, and expect to get jumping-jacks and dolls and a lot of toys that'll be all broken up by the next day. You'll maybe have a tree and hang dingle-dangles on it, and eat turkey and lollipops, and be cross and sick the next day. Christmas isn't all it's cracked up to be by a long shot!

JOE

Yes, we may hang up our stockings, and get some toys in them. But Christmas brings a better gift than any that can be found in stockings, or hung on a tree. Christmas brings the best gift of all.

CHARLIE

What's that?

JOE

The gift of God, which is eternal life! If it hadn't been for Christmas we never could have had that gift at all, and it's the best gift there is.

CHARLIE

How do you make that out? What's Christmas got to do with eternal life? Christmas is a pain in the neck!

JOE

Christmas is *not* a pain in the neck! Why, if Jesus had never been born so He could die for us, there wouldn't have been anything but eternal death for us. It had to be somebody who had never sinned who would die for us, you know. Christmas is the grandest day of all the year, except Easter; that's better yet. Christmas is a birthday, too. The best birthday there is!

CHARLIE

Whose birthday?

JOE

The birthday of a King!

CHARLIE

Who d'ya mean? Santa Claus?

JOE

On no! Not Santa Claus. He's not real. He's just a play character like a fairy. I mean Jesus, the Son of God. Christmas is Jesus' birthday.

A group of girls at the side, whispering and laughing:

He thought Christmas was Santa Claus' birthday! Isn't that funny? Surely he must know better than that!

CHARLIE
(scowling)
How do you know Christmas is Jesus' birthday?

JOE
The Bible tells us so. His whole story is written there!

CHARLIE
Aw, the *Bible!* That's just a book! Somebody wrote it out of his head! It's just imagination!

JOE
(shaking his head wisely)
No, you're all wrong! "Holy men of God spake as they were moved by the Holy Ghost!"

CHARLIE
Where d'ya get that?

JOE
Second Peter, one, twenty-one. Say it, kids!
(He turns to the other children with him.)

ALL
(except Charlie)
"For the prophecy came not in old time by the will of man: but holy men of God spake as they were moved by the Holy Ghost."

CHARLIE
What's the Holy Ghost? How could it move them to speak and write?

DOROTHY
The Holy Ghost is not an *it!* He's a person! He's the same as God. He told the men what to say, just the way the sunshine makes plants grow.

CHARLIE
Aw, that sounds silly! How could He?

JOHN
Maybe it does sound silly to people that don't know Jesus, for the Bible says: "The natural man receiveth not the things of the Spirit of God: for they are foolishness unto him: neither can he know them because they are spiritually discerned." (1 Cor. 2:14)

ANNA
It says, too, that the preaching of the cross is to them that perish foolishness; but to those who are saved, it is the power of God. (1 Cor. 1:18)

ALBERT
Yes, and it says, "If our gospel be hid, it is hid to them that are lost!" (2 Cor. 4:3)

CHARLIE
Well, if I ever heard such nonsense! Who is this Jesus, anyway?

PAUL
He is the Son of God!

ALBERT
He is the Saviour of the world!

ANNA
He is God come down to earth!

CHARLIE
What would God want to come down to earth for?

JOHN
To save us. He had to take on a human body so He could die for us. He is "the Lamb of God which taketh away the sin of the world"! (John 1:29)

CHARLIE
What would He want to save us for?

ELVIRA
Because He loved us.

CHARLIE
How do you know that?

ELVIRA

The Bible says so in John three, sixteen. Say it, kids!

ALL
(except Charlie)

"For God so loved the world that He gave His only begotten Son, that whosoever believeth in Him should not perish, but have everlasting life." (John 3:16)

JOE

We know a song about that! (Joe starts it and all except Charlie sing.) [Tabernacle Hymns Number 2, page 94.]

CHARLIE

Well, save us from what?

ALL shout:
(except Charlie)
S I N!

CHARLIE

I'm not a sinner! I haven't done anything so very dreadful!

DOROTHY

The Bible says "There is none that doeth good, no not one." (Rom. 3 :12)

ANNA
And the Bible says, "All have sinned and come short of the glory of God." (Rom. 3:23)

ANGELINE
It's terrible enough not to be exactly like God. He wants us to be like Him.

MARY
The Bible says "The wages of sin is death, but the gift of God is eternal life through Jesus Christ our Lord." (Rom. 6:23)

CHARLIE
Well, if He calls us sinners, what makes you think He loves us?

MARGARET
The Bible says "God commendeth His love toward us in that, while we were yet sinners, Christ died for us." (Rom. 5:8)

EARLE
It says, "I have loved thee with an everlasting love, therefore with lovingkindness have I drawn thee." (Jer. 31:3)

CHARLIE
Well, what's all this got to do with Christmas anyway, and why on earth does it seem to make you so awful happy?

ANGELINE

Why, away back, two thousand years before Christ was born, God told Abraham that through his seed all the nations of the earth should be blessed. Blessed means happy—and Jesus is the seed promised. And then, about six hundred years before Jesus was born Isaiah told about Him in the Bible. (Isaiah 53) He said He was going to be wounded for our transgressions, He was going to be bruised for our iniquities, that the chastisement of our peace was going to be upon Him, and that with His stripes we were going to be healed. That was a part of the prophecy of how He was to suffer on the cross for our sins. And we are happy because we won't ever have to be punished for our sins.

CHARLIE

Do you mean to say the Bible told all that about Him before He was born?

ANGELINE

Oh yes, and it told a lot more.

ANNA

It told *how* He was to be born, and live and die, and everything about Him. And it all came true, just as it was foretold.

CHARLIE

All right. Let's hear it!

JOE

Okay, kids, let's begin. What say the prophets? Dorothy, you tell him about the first prophecy that a Saviour was going to come.

DOROTHY

It was away back in the garden of Eden, after Satan got into the serpent and talked to Eve, and made her believe that it would be all right to break God's command and eat the fruit, so she ate it and gave some to Adam. And then they were afraid when they heard God call them, because they knew they had sinned. Then God came and talked to them. He said: "What is this that thou hast done?" and He said to the serpent, "Because thou hast done this thou art cursed above all cattle, and above every beast of the field, and I will put enmity between thee and the woman, and between thy seed and her seed; it shall bruise they head, (That meant that Jesus, the seed of the woman, would finally kill Satan) and thou shalt bruise His heel." (That meant that Jesus was to be crucified through the acts of Satan.) That is the first prophecy found in the Bible that the

Saviour was to be one of the future descendants of Eve. It is found in Genesis 3:15.

JOE
What next? Mary, you tell another prophecy.

MARY
Isaiah told that Jesus was to be born of a virgin. You find that in Isaiah 7:14. "Therefore the Lord Himself shall give you a sign; Behold, a virgin shall conceive, and bear a son, and shall call His name Immanuel," which meant, "God with us." That was written seven hundred years before Christ was born.

CHARLIE
And did that come true?

MARY
It certainly did. You find that in the first chapter of Matthew, verses eighteen to twenty-three. Let's all say them, girls!

VIOLET, RUTH, ROSE, MADELINE, MARGARET, EMMA
Now the birth of Jesus Christ was on this wise: When as His mother Mary was espoused to Joseph, before they came together, she was found with child of the Holy Ghost.

Then Joseph her husband, being a just man,

and not willing to make her a public example, was minded to put her away privily.

But while he thought on these things, behold, the angel of the Lord appeared unto him in a dream, saying, Joseph, thou son of David, fear not to take unto thee Mary thy wife: for that which is conceived in her is of the Holy Ghost.

And she shall bring forth a son, and thou shalt call His name Jesus: for He shall save His people from their sins.

Now all this was done, that it might be fulfilled which was spoken of the Lord by the prophet, saying,

Behold a virgin shall be with child, and shall bring forth a son, and they shall call His name Emmanuel, which being interpreted is, "God with us." (Matthew 1:23)

ALBERT
Yes, and the prophet Zechariah told beforehand what would happen when He came. He said He would be sold for thirty pieces of silver. You find that in Zechariah eleven, twelve. "And I said unto them, If ye think good, give me my price; and if not forbear. So they weighed for my price thirty pieces of silver."

EARLE

In Psalm forty-one, nine it was foretold how He would be betrayed by Judas, one of His own disciples. Judas was the one who was paid the thirty pieces of silver by the chief priests. The Psalm says, "Yea, mine own familiar friend, in whom I trusted, which did eat of my bread, hath lifted up his heel against me."

PAUL

Yes, and in John thirteen, eighteen, Jesus reminded them of that. He said, "I speak not of you all. *I* know whom I have chosen: but that the scripture might be fulfilled, 'He that eateth bread with me hath lifted up his heel against me.'"

CLARENCE

Zechariah told, too, how Christ was going to be forsaken by His disciples. Chapter thirteen, verse seven. "Awake, O sword, against my shepherd, and against the man that is my fellow, saith the Lord of hosts: smite the shepherd, and the sheep shall be scattered."

MADELINE

That was fulfilled in Matthew twenty-six, thirty-one. "Then saith Jesus unto them, All ye shall be offended because of me this night, for it is written, I will smite the shepherd, and the sheep shall be scattered abroad."

ERNEST
Verse fifty-six in that same chapter in Matthew shows the fulfillment, too. "But all this was done that the scriptures of the prophets might be fulfilled: 'Then all the disciples forsook Him and fled.'"

CLARENCE
Psalm thirty-five, eleven told that He was going to be accused by false witnesses: It says: "False witnesses did rise up; they laid to my charge things that I knew not."

ALBERT
Yes, and that was fulfilled in Matthew twenty-six, verses fifty-nine to sixty one. "Now the chief priests and elders, and all the council, sought false witnesses against Jesus, to put Him to death, but found none. Yea, though many false witnesses came, yet found they none. At the last came two false witnesses and said, This fellow said, I am able to destroy the temple of God and to build it in three days." They thought He meant the building where they worshipped, but He meant the temple of His body, looking forward to His death and resurrection.

ANNA

Well Isaiah said, in chapter fifty-three, the seventh verse, that He was going to be silent before His accusers. "He was oppressed, and He was afflicted, yet He opened not His mouth. He is brought as a lamb to the slaughter, and as a sheep before her shearers is dumb, so He openeth not His mouth."

PAUL

That was fulfilled in Matthew twenty-seven, thirteen and fourteen. "Then said Pilate unto Him, hearest Thou not how many things they witness against Thee? And He answered them never a word; insomuch that the governor marvelled greatly."

DOROTHY

In Isaiah the fiftieth chapter and the sixth verse, it said He was going to be spit upon and scourged. It says: "I gave my back to the smiters, and my cheeks to them that plucked off the hair. I hid not my face from shame and spitting." And that was fulfilled in Matthew twenty-seven, twenty-six: "Then released he Barabbas unto them: and when he had scourged Jesus, he delivered Him to be crucified." And in chapter twenty-six, verse sixty-seven, "Then they did spit in His face, and buffeted Him."

ANGELINE

Psalm twenty-two, eighteen, told how His garments were going to be parted. It says: "And they parted my garments among them, and cast lots upon my vesture." And it tells in Matthew twenty-seven, thirty-five how that was fulfilled. "And they crucified Him, and parted His garments, casting lots: that it might be fulfilled which was spoken by the prophet, They parted my garments among them, and upon my vesture did they cast lots."

EMMA

In Psalm twenty-two, seven and eight it says: "All they that see me laugh me to scorn; they shoot out the lip, they shake the head saying, He trusted on the Lord that He would deliver Him: let Him deliver Him, seeing He delighted in Him."

ALMA

That was fulfilled in Matthew twenty-seven, forty-one to forty-three: "Likewise also the chief priests mocking Him, with the scribes and elders, said, He saved others: Himself He cannot save. If He be the King of Israel, let Him now come down from the cross, and we will believe Him. He trusted in God; let Him deliver Him now, if He will have Him: for He said, I am the Son of God."

JUNIOR

Psalm sixty-nine, twenty-one, says: "They gave me also gall for my meat; and in my thirst they gave me vinegar to drink."

ALBERT

They did that when He was on the cross. Don't you remember Matthew twenty-seven, forty-eight? "And straightway one of them ran, and took a sponge, and filled it with vinegar, and put it on a reed, and gave Him to drink."

JOE

It was foretold in Psalm twenty-two, one, how God was going to forsake Him: "My God, my God, why hast Thou forsaken me?" And in Matthew twenty-seven, forty-six it tells how that was fulfilled: "And about the ninth hour Jesus cried with a loud voice, saying, Eli, Eli, lama sabachthani? that is to say, My God, my God, why hast thou forsaken me?"

ANTHONY

It was said, too, that He was to die with wicked men. Isaiah fifty-three, twelve: "And He was numbered with the transgressors, and He bare the sin of many, and made intercession for the transgressors."

ANNA
It tells how that was fulfilled, in Luke twenty-three, thirty-two and thirty-three: "And there were also two other malefactors, led with Him to be put to death. And when they were come to the place, which is called Calvary, there they crucified Him, and the malefactors, one on the right hand, and the other on the left."

SAMUEL
Well, it says in Psalm thirty-four, twenty, that His bones were not to be broken. "He keepeth all His bones, not one of them is broken." Was that fulfilled too?

PAUL
Oh, yes, you find that in John nineteen, thirty-two and thirty-three: "Then came the soldiers and brake the legs of the first, and of the other which was crucified with Him. But when they came to Jesus, and saw that He was dead already, they brake not His legs."

CLARENCE
It says in Isaiah fifty-three, nine, that Jesus was appointed to be buried with the wicked, but that He would be with the rich because he

had done no violence; and he *would* have been buried in the potter's field with the two thieves, only a rich man, Joseph of Arimathaea, begged His body of Pilate and buried Him in his own garden. You find that in Luke twenty-three, verses fifty to fifty-three.

CHARLIE
Well, but say, did all these people know about all these prophecies beforehand?

ERNEST
I'll say they did. It was all written in the sacred books, and the whole nation was expecting a Messiah to come some day who would save the people from their sins. Every household was hoping that the child would be born in their home.

CHARLIE
Then I don't see why they crucified Him.

CLARENCE
They didn't recognize Him. Perhaps they didn't listen to the prophecy when it was read in their synagogues. Perhaps they didn't realize He was to be like that. They expected a great king with a jeweled crown and ermine robes. One born in a palace, who would free them from their enemies and make them all wealthy.

They didn't expect Him to be born in a manger, and most of them didn't want the kind of life He offered.

JOE
Yes, you see the people wanted money and power instead of eternal life and goodness. But there were a lot of other prophecies. You haven't told half of them. There were several about His resurrection from the dead.

ARTHUR
Oh yes, Psalm sixteen, ten, says: "For thou wilt not leave my soul in hell"—that means the place of the dead—; "neither wilt thou suffer thine Holy One to see corruption." This is a prophecy that the Lord's body should only remain in the grave three days, because in that land a dead body begins to decay after three days.

SAMUEL
Yes, and Acts two, twenty-five to thirty-one calls that to mind. It quotes that verse and says that David, being a prophet, understood that God would raise up Christ from the dead. And it goes on to say: "He seeing this before spake of the resurrection of Christ, that His soul was not left in hell, neither His flesh did see cor-

ruption." And I've heard that even lawyers say that there is more proof of Christ's resurrection than of any other fact in history.

CHARLIE
Well that certainly is interesting!

JOE
Yes, isn't it? And then, He's *coming* again, you know!

CHARLIE
Coming again? What makes you think that?

JOE
The Bible says so. In Acts one, eleven: "This same Jesus, which is taken up from you into heaven, shall so come in like manner as ye have seen Him go into heaven." That's what the angels said.

DOROTHY
Jesus Himself said He was coming. You find it in John fourteen, three and four: "I go to prepare a place for you. And if I go and prepare a place for you, I will come again, and receive you unto myself, that where I am, there ye may be also."

JOE
Now let's all say First Thessalonians four, sixteen to eighteen.

ALL (except Charlie)
"For the Lord Himself shall descend from heaven with a shout, with the voice of the archangel, and with the trump of God: and the dead in Christ shall rise first: then we which are alive and remain shall be caught up together with them in the clouds, to meet the Lord in the air: and so shall we ever be with the Lord. Wherefore comfort one another with these words."

ANTHONY
Joy and I know a song about that!

JOE
All right, sing it now.

JOY and ANTHONY sing:
I'll Be So Glad

CHARLIE
Say, that's great! But that's a long time ago all that was written! A lot of years have rolled by, and nothing has happened. I guess it doesn't amount to anything nowadays, does it?

DOROTHY

Oh, the Bible even prophesies that people would talk like that. You find it in Second Peter, third chapter. "There shall come in the last days scoffers, walking after their own lusts, and saying, Where is the promise of His coming? For since the fathers fell asleep, all things continue as they were from the beginning of the creation. But, beloved, be not ignorant of this one thing, that one day is with the Lord as a thousand years, and a thousand years as one day. The Lord is not slack concerning His promise, as some men count slackness; but is longsuffering to us-ward, not willing that any should perish, but that all should come to repentance."

JOE

Jesus Christ is the same, yesterday, today, and forever, and God has never broken a promise yet. Sing it, kids!

Joe starts it and they all sing number 235 in "Tabernacle Hymns No. 2," "Yesterday, To-Day, Forever, Jesus Is the Same." (Sing only chorus if preferred.)

CHARLIE

Say, I'd like to get in on this thing myself. How do you do it?

JOE
Just believe on the Lord Jesus Christ and thou shalt be saved.

CHARLIE
Don't ya havta pay anything?

JOE
Not a cent! It's a gift!

ALL (except Charlie) sing
"Jesus Paid It All," Number 288, "Tabernacle Hymns No. 2."

CHARLIE
You mean I could be saved that easy?

JOE
Sure you could! It's all been done for you! John five, twenty-four. Say it, kids!

ALL (but Charlie) recite in unison:
"Verily, verily, I say unto you, He that heareth my word and believeth on Him that sent me, *hath* everlasting life, and *shall not* come into condemnation: but *is passed* from death unto life."

CHARLIE
But wouldn't I have to be judged for my sins?

JOE
No! Jesus has already been judged for your sins, and the sins of the whole world! Second Corinthians five, twenty-one. Say it, kids!

ALL (except Charlie)
"For He hath made Him to be sin for us, Who knew no sin: that we might be made the righteousness of God in Him."

JOE
And first John two, two!

ALL (except Charlie)
"And He is the propitiation for our sins; and not for ours only, but also for the sins of the whole world."

CHARLIE
Then why isn't everybody saved?

ARTHUR
They won't all believe. It says in John three, eighteen: "He that believeth on Him is not condemned, but he that believeth not is condemned already, because he hath not believed on the name of the only begotten Son of God."

CHARLIE
Then I'll believe right now!

JOE
That's grand! (They shake hands.)

JOE (turning to them all)
Let's all sing! (He starts.)

ALL sing (with bowed heads)

> *"Just as I am without one plea,*
> *But that Thy blood was shed for me,*
> *And that Thou bidst me come to Thee,*
> *O Lamb of God, I come, I come!"*

CHOIR sing (in distance)

> *"Ring the Bells of heaven,*
> *There is joy today,*
> *For a soul returneth from the wild"*

or

> *"Joy, joy, joy,*
> *There is joy in heaven with the angels,*
> *Joy, joy, joy,*
> *for the Prodigal returns."*

(Either found in old Gospel Song books.)

CHARLIE
Now I can sing with you, for I am happy too!

All sing as they march to their seats
"I'm So Happy," Number 104 in NEW
PINEBROOK SONGS

How Adelaide Went to the Convention

Praying for a Visitor

"THERE goes that church-bell again! I declare! I'm just about used up, listening to it to-day. I have a nervous headache coming on," said Mrs. Satterlee, as she leaned forward to glance out of the parlor window.

"It is certainly very annoying," assented Mrs. Ashton, another boarder in the same house. "I sometimes wish that we were not located so near the church, except that the church lawn is very pretty to look out upon. It does very well weekdays, but Sunday I'd almost be willing to give that up. How many services they do have nowadays! I should think they would give up some of them this warm weather;" and the lady leaned languidly back, and opened a large fan.

"I should think so!" said the first speaker

energetically. "They are making the Sabbath anything but a day of rest. I don't believe it's right. I believe everybody ought to have a chance to rest and sleep on Sunday; but those young people start up and have their meeting so early that all arrangements have to be changed in order that they may have their tea before they go. I was just in the sweetest sleep this afternoon when that tea-bell jingled. The young people seem to have gone wild over this society of theirs. I'm sure I don't understand it. Tom goes too. I'm glad, of course, to have him take an interest in church-going; still, I wish he would choose some other service. I'm afraid this is doing more harm than good. I tell him he just goes to have a good time. Poor fellow! It has been so dull here this winter that he has to get fun somewhere. The gay young set seems to have quite subsided. They have had no parties this winter to speak of; everything has been this everlasting young people's society. Why, even at their sociables they have all sorts! I don't like it. They mix all classes up too much."

"No," murmured Mrs. Ashton sympathetically; "but I fancy it will be very different when Adelaide returns. She is coming in a week now, and the young people follow her always. She has a magnetic way with her," and the mother smiled a satisfied smile.

The other lady brightened.

"Is Adelaide coming so soon? Well, I am glad. She is such a leader among them, I hope there will be something in the town now besides prayer-meetings. Tom has got it into his head to go off with a lot of them to New York to a meeting of this society. I don't approve of it at all. If it were just a few of the choice young people, I should be willing; but all sorts are going,—anybody in the church that wants to. There are some girls that I don't want Tom with. I call them bold. Why, Mrs. Ashton, they actually get up and lead the meetings, some of them! I say a girl that will do that has lost all self-respect, and I don't want my son mingling with such people, even if they do belong to a church!"

Mrs. Ashton agreed to this, and then said again she was sure Adelaide would create a different state of affairs.

"You know," she went on, "that Adelaide has been in a whirl of gayety all winter, and I'm sure she never will stand it to come home and settle down to the humdrum way in which this town has been moving since that society began. I have written her about things, so she will come home with her head full of plans. Are you going out to church this evening? It is nearly time to get ready. I promised Mr. Ashton I would go around to the hall with him. You know they give a sacred concert there, and take up a collection for the benefit of the Hunt family. We thought we ought to go and help the cause along."

"No, I'm not going out. It is too warm to sit through a sermon to-night. I tried to make Tom think he could take me to the concert, but he says he has promised to go to his own church. Such nonsense! I don't believe in people binding themselves in that way. I'm rather glad he didn't want to go, however, as I'm too tired this evening to keep awake. I hope you'll have a pleasant time."

And the two ladies parted.

In the pretty little stone church opposite, the Christian Endeavor meeting was still going on. They were a young society, but thoroughly in earnest, having had the special blessing of a visit from the national secretary at their start, which had occurred five months before. Also, two young people, a brother and sister, had come among them recently, having moved from a large city church and society. These two, Harold and Enid Burton, had been delegates to the national convention held in Minneapolis; therefore it was not strange that, as they had occasionally told an incident or related a bit of experience belonging to that time, the rest of the society should be enthusiastic on the subject of going to New York. Enthusiasm ran high as the time drew near.

"Adelaide Ashton is coming next week," announced one of the girls at the close of the meeting. "She'll be in time to go with us to New York. Isn't it lovely? I was so afraid she would accept her uncle's invitation for Bar Harbor; but she wrote me yesterday she couldn't stay away any longer: she wanted to get back to us all."

"Will Adelaide go, Cora? You know she never was interested in such things," said another girl doubtfully. Adelaide had been their leader; would she also be willing to be led?

"Neither were we any of us until this winter," responded the hopeful Cora. "If she isn't interested, this will be the quickest way to get her into it. Enid says people can't help getting enthusiastic at the convention. We'll just take her along with us, and you see if she doesn't love the society as much as any of us when we come back."

"You'll have to get her permission first,"

said Tom Satterlee, who lingered on the out-side of the group. He remembered some sharp sentences that Adelaide's mother had spoken about the young people and their prayer-meetings. "She'll have to be very different from what she was when she went away if she doesn't carry us off to something of another character, instead of being carried off to a religious meeting."

"O Tom, don't!" said one of the more quiet-looking girls. "Remember the verse you re-peated to-night: 'For I am persuaded that neither death, nor life, nor angels, nor princi-palities, nor powers, nor things present, nor things to come, nor height, nor depth, nor any other creature, shall be able to separate us from the love of God.' You haven't forgotten that so soon, have you? God can keep us all."

"And Tom," put in Cora in her eager voice, "you forget, too, that the One who has made us all over can make Adelaide over just as easily."

Then Enid's sweet voice said, "Why not all agree to pray for this one soul? I don't know her yet; but I'm interested in her, you have all spoken about her so often. Let us claim that promise: 'If two of you shall agree on earth as touching anything that they shall ask, it shall be done for them.' There are eight of us here, counting my brother. Let us go into the Bible-class room now, just for a minute, and ask Jesus to do this for us. I think there is time before the last bell rings for service."

They had not expected this turn of affairs, and were not ready for it. Tom, at least, would have been glad to be out of it, for he had never prayed aloud in his life. But they followed Enid's motion, and went to the little room close by, while she stepped to her brother's side, and explained the matter to him in a few words.

It was Harold Burton's earnest voice that led in prayer, pleading for the salvation of this soul whom he had never met, yet in whom he was interested because his Elder Brother had died to save her. The petition went all around the little circle of eight. Tom had felt sure that no words would come to him. In the first place, it seemed so queer for him to be kneeling there with the others, when it was barely two weeks since he had learned to pray to God in the privacy of his own room. And then to be praying for Adelaide Ashton, his old schoolmate, the girl who had been able to lead him everywhere, and who had sometimes laughed at him, and called him wild! But as the voices went on pleading the promises, some sense of the greatness of God's power and willingness, and some idea of the worth of a soul, came to him, and he prayed, too, and then wondered at himself, as Enid, who was next to him and last of the circle, took up his words; and his heart echoed every sentence of her prayer.

What would Mrs. Ashton have thought, as she sat in the concert, and complacently mused on the difference that her daughter's home coming would make in the town, could she have known that eight of her daughter's companions, led by the two young people from Chicago, were actually praying for Adelaide? What would Adelaide have felt, who was so sure she could lead them all whither she would, if she could have looked into that Bible-class room and heard the simple, earnest words spoken in her behalf?

"We must hasten," said Enid, as they rose from their knees; "the last bell has almost stopped tolling. I would not have Dr. Masters think we have slipped off home or gone on a walk, as some are getting into the habit of doing."

And with faces that looked as if they had had a sudden uplift, they all went quietly into the church.

2

"Nobody Goes to New York in July"

THEY began to talk about it the first evening after Adelaide reached home. Mrs. Ashton had withdrawn to the other end of the long parlors to entertain callers of her own, so they had it all to themselves. Tom was there, and Cora, and several others who had been Adelaide's intimate friends; but it happened that nearly all of them had been of that little company who had gathered in the Bible-class room to pray for her the week before. They thought of it now as they looked at her, this brilliant, beautiful girl, so full of the world; and they trembled for the answer to their prayers. Tom thought of Enid's prayer that night. Would she have prayed so trustingly if she had known

Adelaide? But the thought of that prayer strengthened Tom's weak faith.

They had rehearsed the winter's doings; at least, Adelaide had done her part, while the rest listened, each mentally comparing their quiet, happy winter of church-work with the gay scene where their friend had passed the last few months.

"And now," said Adelaide, as she finished the story of an interesting experience that she had passed through on the journey, "I've come home with ever so many new ideas and lovely plans. What have you all on hand right away?"

She expected them to declare that they had nothing in the world to do, and were languishing for her to stir them up. The young people she had left in the autumn would have done so, and would have entered with vigor into whatever project she should suggest. But to her amazement she was met by a chorus of, "Oh, the loveliest plan, Adelaide! And we've been so afraid you would not get here in time!"

"Yes, Miss Ashton, you'll have to put off all your plans till this is over, for the girls have to spend every spare minute getting their outfits ready," put in Tom.

This was astonishing, but it sounded interesting. Adelaide thought her mother must have been mistaken when she wrote how dull and stupid the young people had been all winter. Perhaps this was something they had planned especially in honor of her coming home.

"What is it? Do tell me. When is it to be?" she questioned.

"Next week."

"Why, next week is so short a time! Is it to be an elaborate affair? I'm afraid I won't have much time to get ready."

"Oh, yes, you will!" laughed the girls. "Listen; you don't know what it is yet."

"No; but I should judge from what Tom says that it is either a fancy-dress masquerade or a camping expedition."

After the laughter that followed this had somewhat subsided, Cora essayed to explain.

"We are all going to New York," she said.

"To New York!" exclaimed Adelaide. "What in the world are you going there for at this time of year? Winter is the time to take in New York. Why, you must all be crazy! Nobody goes to New York in July."

"You're mistaken there, Adelaide," said Tom as well as he could in the bubble of merriment. "We had a special message that twenty thousand of our friends are to be there at that time, and we are going to meet them."

"Twenty thousand! What do you mean?" exclaimed the astonished young woman. "Tom," severely, "this is one of your absurd jokes, I am sure. I did not think you would begin the very first night."

"Indeed it is not," answered Tom soberly; "I mean every word of it. Twenty thousand, and perhaps more, of our friends and brothers and sisters are going to New York on the seventh of July to meet us, and we expect to enjoy four of the best days we ever spent in our lives."

"Well, really," said Adelaide, "I don't understand how you are going to do it. Have you chartered a special car? Is it a great picnic? Why in the world do you select New York? It will be very hot there. What about chaperons?"

"Why, we are to have a whole train to ourselves, a special train. As for chaperons, I don't believe one of us has thought of them; but Mrs. Burton and Aunt Cornelia and Mrs. Dutton and ever so many other staid people are going along, besides some of the elders of the church, and I suppose you can use them for chaperons; though we haven't considered them in that light before, for they have grown to be one with us so thoroughly this winter that we forgot they were any older than the rest of us," said Tom, smiling to see the astonished look deepen on Adelaide's face. "As for why we go to New York,—why, the committee appointed for the purpose selected that place; and as for the heat, we are all going to take palm-leaf fans," he finished as the rest of the group broke down laughing once more.

"Now, Tom, please be good, and explain to Adelaide," put in Cora, lest the joke might be carried too far. "Tell her why we are going, and all about it."

"We are going to attend the Eleventh Convention of the Young People's Society of Christian Endeavor, and we are all delegates; and you must join us immediately, for really it is going to be the most delightful trip you ever heard of," said Tom, trying to sober down.

Then they all talked at once. It was a long time before they were able to make Adelaide understand. Up to that evening she had had but a vague idea of what the Christian Endeavor Society was; had, indeed, heard its name but a few times. Of its vast proportions, its solemn, binding pledge, and the interest and devotion with which all its adherents regarded it, she heard for the first time. It must be confessed that she began to feel somewhat uncomfortable.

Here were all her friends talking eagerly about things of which she knew nothing, putting into their plans the same energy and life that they had heretofore put into whist parties and private theatricals. What did it all mean? She was rather left out. She resolved at first to decline to join this absurd party who were rushing off to New York to go to meeting. Perhaps this was her opportunity to put things to rights in the town. There was no telling but she might be able to get up an opposition party, and break down the society. She would try it, and see what could be done. Therefore she did not enter into their plan for taking her to New York, but laughed it off, saying she was sure her mother would not hear of her leaving so soon.

The next two or three days, however, showed her plainly that it was much too late for her to attempt to put a stop to this, and she began in spite of herself to become interested. It certainly would be fun to go off on a journey together in the way that they were planning. She would leave things open for a day or two yet. If she found it impossible to get her old friends to change their plans and take their excursion to the seashore instead, it might be as well for her to go and see what there was in this society to attract them all.

Meantime, the quiet Sabbath came on. Adelaide thought it too warm to attend church in the morning, and remained at home till toward evening, when, just as the bell was ringing for the Christian Endeavor service, the little pony and phaeton that she always had from the livery stable, drew up before the door, and she came out dressed in a cool white. Perhaps she lingered purposely in arranging her draperies on the seat and fastening her gloves. Tom Satterlee came out of the door as she gathered up the reins.

She bowed and smiled in a most bewitching manner, and called to him, "Wouldn't you like to take a little drive with me to get cooled off after this fearfully warm day?"

She felt sure that he would be glad to accept her invitation. In the old days it had been said that she could do what she pleased with Tom Satterlee; but to her mortification he only bowed gravely, and said, "Thank you, it has been warm. Our Christian Endeavor meeting is at this hour. I was in hopes we should see you there," and went on across the road.

Adelaide felt too vexed to go on; but she forced herself to take a short drive, pondering meanwhile on what a change had come over this young man. What could it be that attracted them all to the church? She was sorry that she had not gone to see. But she decided during that short, solitary drive, to go to New York. Then she drove home as fast as the pony could carry her, and coaxed her father to go to evening service with her.

"You are absurd, Adelaide!" said her mother the next morning, when that young woman announced her intention of joining the excursion to New York. "I am surprised at you, and disappointed in you. Mrs. Satterlee has been looking to you to keep Tom at home, and here you are giving in the first thing. I should think you would have more spirit than that. You could lead them all if you chose."

"Mamma, you've no kind of an idea how infatuated those girls and boys are. They act like a lot of children going on a Sunday-school picnic, instead of young men and women. I saw it was no use to try to stop it, and so I made up my mind that it was best to go along with them. I can at least cheer their drooping spirits when they are tired of meetings. Besides, they never will go all the time. I'm satisfied that one day will be enough for them, and after that we can go around and have a good time. I'm going to get Tom to take me to the theatre the second night; see if I don't," and she tossed her head in an imperious, pretty little way that always conquered her mother.

"Well, I can't bear to have you go, Adelaide; it seems so common to go in that way, and to New York at this time of year. I do not like to have people think you are infatuated with this thing too."

"Oh, you needn't worry in the least about that. It seems to be quite the fashion, I assure you, though I can't see how it came about; and I am thankful that all my New York friends will be out of town when we are there, so there won't be any embarrassment on that account. Have you seen those Burtons, mamma, who have rented the Parke place? They are quite 'tony' people. The girls had talked so much about that Enid that I was prepared to hate her; but they introduced me last evening, and I must say I liked her. She has a lovely face; and her dress, though very simple and absurdly plain, somehow had a tremendous style about it. The brother is just as handsome as he can be. I was quite taken with him, though he seems just the least bit too grave for a young man. They say they are very rich. Indeed, mamma, I've set my heart on going now, and you need not say no."

3

Endeavor on the Cars

A LARGE company was gathered about the station early in the morning of the day on which they were to start. Those who were not going themselves came down to see the others off. The whole Christian Endeavor Society was there, and among them were faces Adelaide did not know. There was a hum and a buzz. "Has Miss Porter come yet?" was a question that was asked several times before there came the answer of, "Yes; there she is."

"Who, pray, is Miss Porter?" asked Adelaide at last. "I have heard nothing but her name since I came down to the station."

"Why, she is our delegate," answered Enid, who stood near her. "We are all delegates in a sense, you know; but she is our *special* delegate, the one the society is sending. Almost every society sends at least one or two delegates. I wish we could have afforded two. There were some who ought to have gone."

"But I do not remember any Miss Porter. Is she a newcomer here?" asked Adelaide again.

"Oh, no; at least, I think not," responded Enid. "You know I am new myself; but they all speak as if she had been here for years. Here she comes now. Let me introduce Miss Ashton to you, Miss Porter," she said, as a plain-faced girl in a neat gray gingham came toward them.

Adelaide looked up in astonishment. Was it possible that she was being introduced to the girl who had for years made her wash-dresses and done plain sewing for her mother? She favored the special delegate with a half-bow that was mostly stare, and turned coldly to Enid, while little Jane Porter grew suddenly nervous, and almost thought this trip to New York was not so much to be desired as she had supposed. Tom Satterlee came up just then, however, and, bowing respectfully, addressed her as "our honored delegate;" and some of the others gathered around, with their bright cordial words, so that the clouds lifted, and the clear sun shone once more in Jane Porter's world.

Adelaide had received a shock.

"I do not understand," she said to Enid. "Jane Porter never moved in our circle before."

"Did she not?" asked Enid innocently. "Well, isn't it lovely, then, how this Christian Endeavor Society breaks down all barriers, and brings all of God's people together? I was so glad that Miss Porter could go; I think she will enjoy this trip amazingly. Doesn't she look cool and nice in that pretty gingham? I believe she is the most sensible one of our number."

Adelaide looked at Enid's thin wash-silk travelling costume, so very plain, and yet so dainty, and wondered; and then looked down at her own elaborately trimmed wool. This was a new world into which she was entering, and she was not so sure as Enid was that it was all lovely. However, she did not say so.

There was not much time left for speculation. The train was coming. There was bustle and rush; and then, after they were on board, and were waiting for the baggage to be put on, saying the last words to those left behind, through the open car-windows there came the sound of singing started by a group on the platform. It was soon caught up by the whole delegation: "God be with you till we meet again."

The train started while they were still sing-ing; and amid the good-bys and the fluttering handkerchiefs floated back the words,—

"When life's perils thick confound you,
Keep his arms unfailing round you."

And a few astonished brakemen, who were having their first experience in carrying a Christian Endeavor delegation to a national convention, wondered with Adelaide what would come next.

"Harold," said Enid in a low tone to her brother, when they were arranging themselves in the car; "it won't do to have those two together during the journey," and her eyes looked over to where Tom and Adelaide were about seating themselves together. "Tom is afraid of her influence over him, I know, from what he said after meeting the other night. She hasn't the least bit of Christian Endeavor about her yet, I'm afraid, and is disposed to make fun of everything connected with it. I'm almost sorry she has come; for I am afraid she will do more harm than she will get good."

"Yes; I saw the way she treated Miss Porter. Abominable, wasn't it? But don't say that, little sister; you know we have claimed a promise.

You are right in regard to those two, however; they must be kept apart. Will you look out for Tom? He likes you pretty well, and I know you have a knack of making it pleasant for the boys when you try. I'll undertake to discover whether Miss Ashton and myself have a single interest in common, though I must say I don't enjoy the prospect. Perhaps there is more to her than there looks to be."

And so it came about presently that Tom Satterlee, instead of spending his morning with Adelaide, making jokes, and hearing her sharp sarcasm flung at the poorer members of their company, and at "fanatics"—as she called them—in general, found himself beside Enid Burton, having a bright, pleasant talk, which presently turned, of itself it seemed, to subjects more serious, which had lately become dear to his heart. He liked Enid none the less because she was able and willing to talk about Jesus Christ as freely and happily as about worldly things. The morning's conversation was always remembered as one of the most helpful of his whole life.

Harold and Adelaide did not get on quite so well. The points of harmony between them were difficult to discover, it appeared.

"I shall try to find out of what sort that

handsome Mr. Burton is, the very first thing," she had told her mother before she left home; and so she set about it.

Harold called her attention to the scenery rushing by them so rapidly. There was a bird of rare coloring, then a flower by the wayside, or the sparkling of the dew in the fields, where the spiders had spread their delicate webs to bleach, perhaps. He quoted a lovely bit of a poem about the woods, as they passed swiftly through a cool, thick grove; but although she listened and admired him for it, she felt out of her element. These were not things she had thought about or talked of much. She never saw anything in the trunk of a tree more than some ugly gray bark. She could not talk of the wonders of nature, because she knew nothing about them. He tried books; but their reading had been in so entirely different lines that, with the exception of "The Casting Away of Mrs. Lecks and Mrs. Aleshine," and one or two sparkling bits of humor that have become popular, they found no common ground in the field of literature. Harold paused a moment to consider what to take up next, and Adelaide rose to the occasion.

"Speaking of Shakespeare, Mr. Burton, I suppose you have seen all his plays, have you not? I have never had the opportunity of seeing Booth play them. I am just dying to see him. I hope we shall have an opportunity while we are in New York. Do you know what plays are to be there this week?"

"No, I do not," answered young Burton.

"I have not been to New York since I was a very small child, and I anticipate a good many things that one is not able to get in other places. Don't you think they have very inferior amusements in our town? I suppose it has been as usual this winter. Have there been any plays worth anything?"

"I really cannot tell you, Miss Ashton; I never attend the theatre," said the young man, who, in spite of the poor success he was having, could not but laugh at the difference between himself and this young woman. Yet she was bright and intelligent. Why was it? Would not this soul be worth winning for the Master? He would try; and with a prayer for help he threw his whole heart into an effort to interest her. The first subject that came to his mind was athletics. Yes, to be sure, Miss Ashton was interested in college athletics and in tennis. What young woman is not pleased to hear an account of college days and contests? She was a good tennis-player also, and could speak in scientific terms about the game, could even understand and appreciate when he told her of the old tennis-courts of other days, and the mathematical calculation required in playing the game as it was then played. He spoke, too, of the knights of the tennis-court, and of their oaths. Harold Burton sighed, and wished he could lay out a tennis-court there in the car; for then he might hope to interest this girl, and acquire an influence over her for higher things.

But this was not a young man who liked to spend a whole morning in the company of an immortal soul, and never let it be known by word or action that he had thoughts for a life beyond this one. There were friends who said Harold Burton was too grave, and brought in religious subjects too much in his conversation, repelling people before he had gained an influence over them. It may be so, but then the Lord almost always brought success to this young man's efforts. Perhaps the Holy Spirit taught him how to speak words that should not offend.

He spoke of Christian Endeavor now, and little by little the conversation became more personal. He asked her why she was not an active member instead of an associate.

"Oh, dear me!" she responded. "I've no interest in such things."

"You do not mean you have no interest in Jesus Christ?" he said.

Surely, this was a strange specimen of a young man! Adelaide had never been so embarrassed before in her whole life. Finally she looked up, and answered daringly, "I'm sure I don't know. How should I be interested in some one who lives away off up in the sky somewhere? I am not interested in far-away things."

"Oh, but Jesus Christ is not far away! He is very near his children all the time. He is very dear to me. I wish you knew him."

This seemed all so strange to Adelaide. What was she to say?

"Won't you think about it, Miss Ashton?" went on the quiet, pleasant voice before she could frame a reply. "And may I add your name to the list of those I am praying for? I should like to have you know Christ."

She murmured some sort of thanks, she hardly knew what. Then as quietly and easily as he had dropped into this subject, this strange young man glided into other and less embarrassing topics, talking in an animated, interesting way until she regained her self-possession, and to a certain degree her spirits.

At last Adelaide thought it was time to change the order of the hour.

"Wouldn't you like to have a game?" said she. "Your sister and Mr. Satterlee will join us, I am sure. Tom," leaning across the aisle to speak to him, "won't you and Miss Burton come over and have a game of whist with us? I have my pack of cards with me"; and she produced a pack of cards in a daintily engraved silver case.

In spite of himself, as Harold Burton looked upon the cards there went over in his mind that Bible verse about the sons of God being met together and Satan coming also. And he smiled to think how powerless those bits of pasteboard were to fight against Christ's cause just then, even in the hands of that lovely girl.

Her First Meeting

THERE was dismay and embarrassment in Tom's face; but before he could reply, Enid leaned forward, and said in her cheery tone, "Thank you, Miss Ashton, but neither my brother nor I play cards; and, besides, we were just about to start some singing, and we need your help. I've heard a great deal about your voice. Here is a book. You won't find the music difficult, even if you are not familiar with the selections. We are going to sing 'Blessed Assurance.' You must have heard it."

Almost before she knew it, Adelaide found a singing-book substituted for her cards, while the sweet song swelled all about her. She felt chagrined, and shut her lips, firmly resolved not to sing a word; but the clear tenor voice by her side tempted her to join the rest. It struck her as a very queer thing to do, this singing on the cars; but the whole expedition was queer. She heartily sympathized with the amazed looks of brakemen and conductors.

There seemed to be no further opportunity for the silver card-case to reappear. Indeed, as the journey progressed, there were moments when Adelaide wished she might retire into obscurity with it, she felt so utterly out of harmony with her environment.

A prayer-meeting on the cars! It seemed irreverent when one thought of it; and yet the young woman could not but admit that there was the utmost reverence in the faces of all when, as darkness settled down upon the fast-moving landscape, they gathered, as many as could, in one car for a half-hour's service. Adelaide decided that Harold Burton would make a fine-looking minister if he would wear a gown as they did in many city churches. As for what he had said when he stood in the aisle near her, and spoke those few earnest, ringing sentences, which could be heard even above the rumble of the train, she straightway tried to forget that, because it reminded her uncomfortably of his morning's talk with her.

Before they separated to their berths for the night, the train stopped a few moments at a large town, and the whole company broke into song. Cabmen and railroad men gathered about the platform, and with lifted hats and bowed heads acknowledged their respect for the Jesus Christ about whom the Endeavorers were singing. Adelaide watched them curiously from her window; and just as the train was in motion again, passing slowly by the crowds of men, one old bent man caught her eye, and bowing low said, "God bless you for that song, miss!"

Adelaide was startled once more. She had not realized that her own voice was helping on the song. It was a new experience to be thanked by such a poor fellow-mortal; and yet it was not an unpleasant sensation.

> *"Was it for crimes that I have done*
> *He groaned upon the tree?"*

they had sung. It was easy to feel that the old man's crimes had been their theme, and yet she had a dim sense that she was not wholly guiltless. It was an uncomfortable feeling. She had always been right, in her own opinion. Was it possible that she had helped to preach a gospel of which she knew nothing?

All too soon the journey ended; for not-

withstanding there had been various unexpected delays during the night, the time had
seemed short.

Adelaide drew a sigh of relief as they prepared to leave the cars for the ferry-boat.
Civilization was reached at last, once more,
and now surely eccentricities would be forgotten. The past few hours were well enough
for a lark, but had been rather a strain upon
her nerves.

It appeared that there was need for hurry,
the train was so late, and therefore they agreed
to register at their headquarters, and go at
once to the opening meeting.

Adelaide did not like the arrangement. She
preferred to have her trunk, and a chance for rest,
before making her *début* in New York. She threw
out various pointed hints to Tom Satterlee, to the
effect that she would like to be escorted to their
stopping-place instead of to Madison Square; but
Tom doggedly refused to take any hint. He felt
out of patience to think that this girl had come
when she did not care for the meetings. Adelaide
meditated asking Harold Burton to take her to
the hotel, but the eagerness he expressed in
hoping they might get into the meeting made
her afraid to attempt it. There was nothing for it
but to rush with the rest.

"It is absurd," she murmured to Cora, when they finally jammed into a crowded car. "What are they in such a hurry about? It is not quite time for the meeting to open, and it would not hurt them if they did miss a few words."

"But they are afraid we cannot get in," panted long-suffering Cora.

"Nonsense!" said Adelaide sharply; "they don't know what they are talking about. That building is tremendous. I've read all about it. There won't be half enough to fill it, you may depend on it;" and she straightened up with a superior air.

Cora looked at her half pityingly, and was silent.

Arrived at Madison Square Garden, this confident, eager party were confronted on every side by crowds of disappointed people, and by imperturbable policemen.

"It is full," said the officers of the law. "Not another one can come in."

"I don't believe it," said Adelaide, suddenly becoming anxious to get in. "They have no right to shut us out when we have come so far."

They tried all the doors with no better success, and Adelaide grumbled all the way.

You would certainly have thought her main interest in life for the past few years had been to get into that meeting. They went to their hotel then, resolved to profit by experience, and be on time for the evening.

Adelaide felt so out of patience with the authorities for not having made arrangements for them to get into the hall, that she was disposed to stay away altogether that evening, perhaps to make the management feel sorry; but she found that there was not one of their party willing to remain with her unless she was absolutely ill, and she would not stay alone in a New York hotel, so she put on her martyr air and went, mentally resolving that the next evening should find her on the way to a theatre instead of a meeting.

Seated in the Garden at last, and with a breathing-space before the services opened, Adelaide had opportunity to look about her. What a sea of people in every direction, and more coming all the time! She began to have some dim conception of what a mighty army of Christians this society could muster. It seemed to her as if the whole world was before her; and she had said there would be "nobody" in New York! But there was no time to reflect on it now. The great electric C.E.

flashed out over the platform, bringing loud applause from the audience. It did not mean the same to this girl that it did to most of those gathered there. She had no precious thoughts in connection with it, of how we are "workers together with God," "endeavoring" inside of "Christ." The monogram simply meant to her the name of the society; but it was as if the light of those letters had flashed the symbol out from God, acknowledging to the world the heavenly calling of this great company. And she was a part of it! A part, and yet not one of them! She began to feel again that great uneasiness of mind which had troubled her twice before since she left home. Her soul, unused to thrilling over anything greater than a lovely dress, or fine music or acting, began to feel the great power of this vast assemblage, and swelled with new thoughts and feelings, until it seemed as if she must cry or faint, or do some silly, childish thing just to bring herself back to realities once more. The wonderful singing choked her. She could not join in it; for it seemed as if she were being borne upward by the music to meet eyes so holy that her being shrank, and longed to go away and hide. She sat and listened, but heard not much, her mind being too full to take in any more.

When the president came forward, and was greeted by voice and hand and handkerchief, and all the other ways the audience could find to express their deep love and joy, Adelaide roused a little, and said, "Who is he?"

And Harold Burton, who sat next, said with shining eyes and glowing countenance, "He is our dear president, who put us all to work in the first place."

How that audience cheered! How eagerly and freely they expressed their admiration and approval! If Mrs. Ashton had been there, she might have pronounced it "out of place," or "quite rude and plebeian," or some other conventional phrase. Her daughter was too much shaken to do so. She could only look and wonder and listen. The meeting was sufficiently extraordinary to all present; but to this girl, who had never even attended a Christian Endeavor prayer-meeting, it was so strange and wonderful that she was almost stunned by it. She did not quite recover her equilibrium until she and her friend Cora were in their room in the hotel.

Enid and Miss Porter roomed next, and the communicating door between the two rooms stood open. The girls talked as they went about their preparations for the night.

"Will you go to the sunrise prayer-meeting, Adelaide?" questioned Cora.

"No, I will not," snapped Adelaide in a decided tone; "and you'll be a goose if you go. It is just dissipation to go so much. I think it is just as bad to dissipate in religion as anything else. The idea of going to a prayer-meeting at that unearthly hour. You'll be down sick. I shouldn't think of doing such a thing."

"Why, Adelaide, I have stayed up all night until nearly that hour many a time in my life, and so have you, and danced most of the time too. I don't believe it will be any worse for me to get up a little earlier than usual and go to a quiet prayer-meeting."

Adelaide subsided soon, declaring that she did not wish to be disturbed in the morning; but somehow when the morning did come her eyes were as wide open as any one's, and sleep seemed impossible.

"O Miss Ashton, you are awake, aren't you?" asked Enid Burton, tiptoeing softly in, and finding Adelaide raised half-way, and resting on one elbow; "do get up and go with us to the meeting. I'm sure you will enjoy it. You've plenty of time, for Harold just knocked at my door to waken me. Come, let me help you dress."

Something in Enid's persuasive tone impelled Adelaide to comply without a word. It was very strange for her to do it, but she could not seem to help it.

Cora stared, and Tom Satterlee drew a long, low whistle as Adelaide and Enid met them in the hall below a few minutes later; but they were not much more surprised than was Adelaide herself, to think that she was actually going of her own free will to a prayer-meeting before breakfast.

"This is all your doing. I congratulate you on your extraordinary success, Miss Burton," whispered Tom to Enid.

"Not a bit of it," answered Enid quickly; "I have done nothing. Do you forget to whom we have been praying, and what promises we have pleaded?"

"I am afraid I did," answered Tom humbly, as they entered the hall together.

5

The Consecration Meeting

THE PRECIOUS morning meeting, which was so helpful to the delegates present, filled Adelaide with a nameless feeling, half dread, half awe. By breakfast-time this had developed into a genuine fit of bad temper. She was out of sorts to think that she had been coaxed into going out so early, and had been compelled to entertain serious thoughts for a time.

All the talk at the table was of the meetings and the programme that was before them. Adelaide took little part in the conversation, and soon went to her room, declaring her intention to write to her mother. But somehow the sarcastic sentences that she had planned to write did not reel off so easily. A sudden dread of being left alone with the entire morning on her hands possessed her;

and, seizing her hat and gloves, she rushed out after the others, who had started to the morning meeting; even the novels that she had brought along to while away the hours seemed distasteful to her.

She was received without comment, despite the fact that she had said she could not think of attending a meeting that was to be all reports; that she hated business of any sort. The pastor's hour was interesting. No one could help listening; and there was such an air of cordial freedom in the great meeting that one did not soon grow weary.

When the one-minute reports from the States began, Adelaide looked about her company to see whether they were not restless, and ready to go on some pleasure excursion; but there was breathless eagerness expressed in every face. So she settled back to endure, and presently became as absorbed as any one. What a tremendous enterprise this was which filled the minds of all about her! How they had grown! And what was the secret of all their enthusiasm? These were thoughts that surged through her brain as one report followed another.

Alaska's name was called. Adelaide looked about in astonishment. Could it be possible that there was a society in that far country?

Surely not! What absurdity to think such a thing! But even as she thought, a young Alaskan Indian was introduced from the platform.

"Isn't he cute?" she said to Cora, after an instant's critical survey. And Cora began to wonder why she had ever admired this girl; but Enid Burton was looking for answers to prayers, and was glad to see even this small amount of interest manifested, and she said in a low, eager tone, "Yes, he is; and oh, isn't it wonderful?"

Adelaide studied curiously for a moment the sweet, earnest face beside her, and then let her eyes and thoughts go back to the platform. The speeches were all so brief that one had scarcely time to recover from the astonishment and delight over one report before another equally remarkable was in progress. A young lady from Spain came to the platform, and every head was stretched to see as they listened to the few words from old Spain.

"The idea!" exclaimed Adelaide, as she stretched her neck with the rest. It was really becoming quite interesting. Indeed, she was not quite sure that the convention was so very plebeian, after all; for a young Englishman spoke, and a young man from Australia. This novice delegate began to feel quite as if her mind were being improved by seeing all the

strangers from abroad. And the wonders mul-
tiplied. India was heard from, and China, and
Africa, and even old Mexico. Then there came
a perfect whirl, so that the audience ceased to
be amazed at anything, even when a whole
delegation arose, responding to something
with cheers or songs or recitation in concert.

Adelaide's nerves were wrought up to such
an extent by noon, that she declared that
nothing would soothe them but a shopping
excursion. She found another member of their
party who was influenced by necessity rather
than choice to accompany her, and meetings
were put out of her mind for a time. All the
afternoon, much to the annoyance of the
other member of the expedition, the shopping
was prolonged. Adelaide revelled in the sight
of beautiful fabrics and exquisite colorings,
while her companion would have been glad
to hasten through her purchases and make an
attempt to get into the afternoon meeting.
Her hopes in that direction were vain, however, as she very soon perceived. Adelaide Ashton was in her element again, and meant to
stay there as long as possible. She looked at
everything she wanted—and did not want;
and she bought a long pair of delicate evening
gloves, a cobweb of a handkerchief at a fabu-

lous price, and a five-pound box of Huyler's best,—this last with which to sweeten the members of her party toward their renegade delegate. Then they took an ice at a fashionable restaurant, and went back to their hotel. Her spirits had risen as the afternoon progressed. She felt in the sunniest mood possible, and passed her bonbons with a free hand and bewitching smiles.

On the way home she had been forming a plan, which was to coax Tom Satterlee to take her to the theatre that evening. She went about the task with much tact, using all the old arts that had always worked with Tom before. Tom was almost caught, and forgot for a time how much he feared the influence of this girl. She did look charming to-night.

But when at last he understood what she wanted, his face clouded over, and his heart gave a great bound of warning. It seemed ungentlemanly in him to say that he was unwilling to leave the meeting, and he was afraid that his new convictions on the subject of theatre-going would not stand the fire of this girl's sarcasm.

"But the meeting, Adelaide; have you forgotten?" he ventured to ask.

"No, I have not," said Adelaide petulantly.

"Haven't you had meeting enough for one day? I'm sure I've had enough to last for a year."

It certainly was trying to have Tom act so when she had thought him on the point of yielding. She added a little more persuasion. He was an old friend, and she felt at liberty to do so.

Tom looked troubled. What if he should go for this once? It would be a trial to miss the great meeting; but how was he to get out of it? It seemed impossible to explain. He looked down; but the gleam of reflected light from the letters of his gold badge seemed to try to attract his attention. A thrill of joy filled him as it had the evening before when the letters flashed out from the platform. He remembered that the Christ for whom he was endeavoring was always there ready to put his strong arms about his weak efforts, just as the "C" of the pin was surrounding and upholding the "E." He looked up with firm determination.

"Adelaide," said he,—and she thought there was more nobleness in his face than she had ever seen there before,—"I'm sorry not to please you, but I cannot do this. You know, perhaps, that I have just given myself to Jesus Christ. I have promised to do as he would have me throughout my whole life, just so far as I know how. I'm not very wise about these things yet, and probably couldn't answer your arguments; but I feel sure of one thing, having thought it over carefully, and that is, that the One whom I have promised to serve would be better pleased if I did not attend the theatre; and so I have decided not to go any more. But, Adelaide, go to the meeting with me. Come! you will enjoy it, I know."

Adelaide had it in her heart to sneer at him, to try to laugh him out of this fanatical state of mind; but something in his face kept her quiet. It was the same look that Enid wore all the time, the look that had shone in Harold Burton's face when he spoke those few earnest sentences to her on the train. What was it that made them all so alike? She looked at Tom for a moment with a new respect for him dawning in her heart.

"What has got hold of you all since I went away? I cannot understand it in the least," she said in a puzzled tone quite different from her former manner.

"It is Jesus Christ, Adelaide; and oh! I wish he would take hold of you too," said Tom with a sudden earnestness of desire that brought courage with it.

The girl had no reply ready. She was nearer to crying than she could remember to have been since her childhood. She looked steadily out of the window for several minutes, until others came over to them and spoke to Tom. She slipped away then, and soon stood with the rest in the hall, ready for meeting. That was her final surrender to the power of the meetings. She went to everything thereafter as a matter of course.

Perhaps she did not enjoy that evening's rare treat as did some others, for her mind was busy with a great problem; though to a certain extent she did enjoy it, and told Tom condescendingly on the way home that it was almost as interesting as the theatre. But what had so changed Tom Satterlee? Constantly during the evening Adelaide asked herself this question; and as often came Tom's words, "It is Jesus Christ."

> *"What a wonderful Saviour is Jesus, my*
> *Jesus!*
> *What a wonderful Saviour is Jesus, my*
> *Lord!"*

sung the great audience; but this girl did not feel the power of his name.

"Blessed assurance, Jesus is mine,"

rang out the song as the company surged out
of the hall; and she looked in this face and that,
and saw that there was a blessed assurance in
each of those hearts. She saw the curious, and
in some cases almost wistful, look in the faces
of the stalwart policemen who stood at the
doors, looking and listening; and the thought
came to her that she and those policemen
were together outside this great throng.

The great Saturday-morning missionary
meeting opened a new world to many present;
but to Adelaide it was so new that she scarcely
could breathe in its high, fine air. Why, what
sort of talk was this of giving money and time
to God, and speaking of it not only as a duty,
but as a privilege? When the missionaries and
native Christians from the different countries
spoke of the great companies of people who
had not heard of Jesus, she felt condemned
that she was worse than they, for she had at
least heard of Jesus. Yet she did not know him.
She and the policemen and the heathen! Fine
company, truly, for Adelaide Ashton!

They all visited the Eden Musée for an hour
that afternoon, and looked at the marvellously
lifelike waxwork. But not even this could

draw Adelaide's mind from the great subject that had taken possession of her; for the "Chamber of Horrors" was filled with reminders of death, and, turn which way she would, the thought was brought to her that she had made no preparation for the end of life. She came away tired and nervous.

The Sabbath dawned, that wonderful Sabbath, when it seemed as if God was so near to New York. None of the delegates ever spent such a day, or ever expect to see another just like it.

Adelaide went to church in the morning with the others. She had progressed so far that it did not seem queer and out of order when the waiting audience broke into song before the service. She was as willing to hurry as any one at noon, and sat through the long afternoon service without once suggesting that they should leave. Something strange and new, which she did not understand, had possession of her. Some of the addresses seemed burned into her very soul. Now they filled her with sorrow and shrinking, and now with great longing.

At last came the crowning meeting of all,— the solemn consecration meeting.

It was with difficulty that Harold Burton had succeeded in getting his party into the hall that night, for the throng gathered long before the hour, and filled the streets.

"And we *must* get in for the farewell meeting," they said. "There will be seven or eight simultaneous meetings, and some must go to those; but oh, do let us get into the hall if possible!"

It seemed as if the hall had grown larger, and the police must have stretched the law a little, for the heads were certainly more numerous than before; and when the great throng sang, it was as one might think would sound the music of the hundred and forty and four thousand.

> *"But remember, this same Jesus*
> *In the clouds will come again,"*

sang the company.

Harold Burton leaned toward Adelaide, and said in a low voice, "What if he should come to-night, Miss Ashton, with us all assembled? Wouldn't it be wonderful?" Perhaps he forgot for the instant what sort of girl this was, or it may be that God's Spirit was moving him to speak.

"Oh, don't!" said she, shivering, and pressing her hands over her eyes, trying to shut out the dreadful thought.

All through that wonderful meeting she sat listening to the united voice of the delegations' consecration words or songs, her heart swelling with strange longing to be one with them, to give herself to Christ as they were doing.

She had taken her hat off with the other ladies in the audience when the request came from the leader; and she sat there in the most plebeian way, bare-headed, on a Sabbath evening, at a religious service in the city of New York. Her mother would have been shocked.

At the close, when Dr. Clark called for all the active members of the Christian Endeavor Society to rise, in dismay Adelaide looked about upon this army of Christians, and felt herself alone. No one else was seated near her. Must she be left out? She covered her face with her hand a moment, it seemed so solemn and awful a time. It was with true joy that she heard that other earnest, pleading invitation given to all the rest to come to Jesus. It seemed all for her, and she felt that it came from the Master himself. Quietly, timidly, with downcast eyes, she stood beside Harold and Enid Burton. But there was another pledge to be made. Would each one of that great company promise by the lifting of the hand to try to bring at least one soul to Christ during the year? Would Adelaide? Oh, *could* she? That was her question. She would gladly do it; and up came her hand with all that forest of other hands, each meaning an immortal soul for Jesus.

Adelaide had risen so quietly in her place, at a time when the others were intent upon their own pledges, that only Harold and Enid noticed that she was standing with them. Enid's arm stole softly about her, and Harold bent low to murmur, "What a wonderful Saviour is Jesus, my Lord."

The little company of friends went out from that meeting with gladdened hearts, and with faith ashamed of its weakness, when they found what God had wrought among them. Jesus Christ was stronger than they trusted him to be. He was able even to lead Adelaide Ashton to himself.

And Adelaide has gone home to work for her one soul as she pledged; and she will still be the leader among her young friends, though in a different way from the one that her mother planned.

Why Adelaide Stayed Home
from the Convention

The Mother in Montreal

THE WINTER had been a bright one for the Christian Endeavor Society of Medway, all too short for the earnest work that had been crowded into its few months; and now at last the summertime was coming again, and with it the longed-for convention in Montreal. They had talked of it all winter, the whole society, and especially those that had been to New York. It is true that the distance this year would be greater and the expense larger; but in spite of these drawbacks this society meant to have a larger delegation than ever. With the exception of one beloved member, who had left them to attend the great convention that shall never break up, the entire delegation of the year before was planning to go. Of the whole number the most eager and interested one in all the planning had been Adelaide Ashton.

It was a daily marvel to some of her friends to watch this young Christian's growth. Born into the kingdom of heaven at the last convention, her heart looked forward to the coming one with eagerness and longing. To be once more in that great company of young followers of her new Master, to join with them in singing and in prayer, and to feel herself one with them—she could scarcely wait for the time to come. All winter long she had been working with others to get together money that there might be many of their society sent; for she felt that to others also might the sweet message come in this way, just as it had come to her soul a year ago. Systematically they had laid aside money for the purpose,—all they could spare without robbing the Lord's treasury in other directions; and many friends had been coaxed to contribute to the good cause, until the fund had swelled and swelled, and they were able to send and pay the expenses of several delegates that would not otherwise have been able to go. Now at last the time was drawing near. Most of the arrangements had been made, and all was moving as it had been planned.

A special meeting of the society had been called to settle some matters connected both with society interests and with the plans for the trip, and this meeting was just breaking up amid much eager talk, as usual.

"Oh, isn't it grand, Adelaide?" exclaimed one of the younger girls. "I'm really to go. I've wanted to go more than any other thing in life for this summer, and at last mamma has promised to let me give up my trip to the mountains and go."

Adelaide smiled, and put her arm lovingly around the pretty girl, and said she was glad. Adelaide had grown to be a great favorite with the younger girls during the winter, and, indeed, with every one. Her mother said she was making herself too common, and she was disappointed in her daughter; but other people said, "What a change has come over Adelaide Ashton! I wouldn't know her for the same girl she was last year. There is no sweeter character in the place now, and she used to be so haughty and exclusive."

Others crowded about, and began to ask questions.

"Adelaide, mamma wanted me to ask you what would be most suitable and comfortable to wear on the journey," said one.

The young woman of the year before would have advised a heavy, tailor-made travelling suit, or else a dainty wash-silk, with furbelows innumerable; but this girl only said, "Your gray gingham, Fannie, by all means. It will be cool, and keep clean till you get there, and I would not spoil a nice dress. Besides, that is very pretty. I'm going to wear a gingham myself."

Perhaps it was this sentence, together with the sweet, bright smile that accompanied it, that gave courage to the quiet, sad-faced girl on the outer edge of the group to come nearer and make a request that had been swelling in her heart during the evening.

"Miss Ashton, may I speak with you just one moment before you go, when they are through with you?" she said.

"Why, certainly," said Adelaide with another smile. "Girls, will you excuse me? You don't need me any longer, anyway. You know as well as I how to answer your own questions. Come over here, Miss Mould, and we shall not be interrupted," and she led the way to a classroom near the door.

"Are you not going with us to Montreal?" she asked, to begin the conversation, as the girl did not seem ready to speak.

"Oh, I'd give a thousand dollars to go, if I had it!" exclaimed Lettie Mould, the tears suddenly springing to her eyes; "but I know it's impossible. I couldn't afford it; and if I could, it's the busy season at the workrooms. Why, I could hardly get off for the meeting to-night, for we have to sew almost every evening now; but I felt I must come just to ask this favor of some one. Of course I couldn't get off at such a time if I could go; and anyway I couldn't leave Annie, for she's sick so much, and her work is so hard on her, I have to help her out very often; and if any one went to see mother, it ought to be Annie, you know, because she's sick, and she's the youngest. But excuse me, Miss Ashton, you don't know. Our mother lives there in Montreal, and I was wanting to ask whether you would mind carrying a letter and a few little things to her. Of course we could send them by mail; but you know it does one so much good to hear by another's lips about their dear ones; and I've been thinking, if it wouldn't be too much trouble, if you could just go and see her, and tell her we're well, and a little about us, it would be such a comfort to us and to her. You see, mother has been sick; and she can't sell the house, and we've had bad luck trying to get money together to send up for her coming to us, as Annie's been sick and needed so much medicine and doctors; but we're just breaking our hearts for a sight of her, and it's been nearly a year since we left;" and the tears rolled down her thin, tired cheeks as she tried to suppress a sob.

Adelaide put her arms about the girl, trying to comfort her. She promised to go and see her mother, and to take all the messages they could send; and she wished with all her heart that she had known this an hour before, so that she might have proposed Lettie Mould as the last delegate, in place of the one she had suggested. But the sexton was turning out the lights, and the young people at the door were calling loudly to her to come. There was no time for more talk now, so, with added promises and a tender, comforting kiss, Adelaide said good-night.

But though there was much interesting talk on the way home, Adelaide's mind was absorbed with perplexing thoughts. She could not get away from that girl's sad face when she said, "We're just breaking our hearts for a sight of her."

Was there nothing she could do to brighten the burden of this other daughter of her King?

She thought of it long after reaching her room that night. Various plans began to form themselves; but they all seemed impractical, and had to be abandoned, until at last, just as she was closing her eyes with a sigh that there absolutely was no way in which she could help Lettie Mould to go to Montreal, a way opened up clearly before her, so startlingly simple, and yet involving such tremendous personal sacrifice, that she opened her eyes wide, and sat up to think it over.

2

"Inasmuch"

I COULDN'T possibly do it," she said to herself as she stared at the moonlight. "What would they all say? Mamma, too, would think me dreadful, for she is quite in favor of my going this year. I'm afraid she would feel badly about it. I've promised to take care of Lucy Townsend,—though I know Cora could do that as well as I,—and I couldn't give it up. Oh, I couldn't do that! It wouldn't be right for me to give up the convention; I need it so much to help me for the next year. And I have felt that I was to meet Jesus Christ again almost face to face, as I did last year. I know he can meet me here just as well as in Montreal; but oh, he seemed so near in that great company! Would he have me stay away?"

She covered her face with her hands, and

began to think it over, then suddenly slipped from the bed to her knees. If only all Christ's children would go to him immediately with any perplexing question or trouble of conscience, there would not be so much time spent in worry and doubt as there now is. This young disciple had early learned the simple way of going straight to her Master in all times of doubt. Face to face with her Saviour, everything stood out clearly, and what had before seemed uncertain was now plain as day. There was no longer any doubt in her mind what he would have her do, and the only question left was whether she was willing to do it.

Then there came to Adelaide an uplift, the echo of his own dear voice speaking sweet words to her, "Inasmuch . . . to one of the least of these," and "unto me." The old words, only fuller, richer, deeper, and meaning more than those words had ever meant to her before. Was it a touch of his hand, with a blessing, that brought such a sense of his presence, and made her feel she would gladly, gladly, make this sacrifice? Sacrifice? Why, it was no longer that! It was happiness to be able to give up something for his dear sake.

When she rose from her knees, the moonlight in her room seemed to have grown brighter, and her heart felt lighter than it had even in view of the expected pleasure she had just determined to surrender. It was not that there was no longer any pleasure to her in the thought of the trip she had planned, or that there would not come to her moments of extreme pain and disappointment over her loss of the good time; but now she had been talking with Jesus, and her heart was lifted far above mere selfish pleasure. When the regrets came, she would bear them; she would take them to her Comforter, and he would bear them for her; but now she was thinking of what he would have her do, and her thoughts grew quite eager in planning how all the stones should be rolled out of this new path that she had chosen to walk in.

There was much thinking to be done immediately; for if Lettie Mould was to go to the convention in her place, there was need of haste.

Adelaide remembered that Lettie had said that there were reasons why she could not get away, even if she could afford to go. Her invalid sister Annie had been the first.

"Well," said Adelaide meditatively, "that certainly need not stand in the way. If I'm not able to take care of that girl, and help her with her work, and amuse her a little besides, for a week, I'm not worth much. I've nothing else in the world to do; at least, nothing else I ought to do. It's in a perfectly respectable neighborhood, and the house she boards in is clean and neat; so mamma cannot object, though I'm very sure she will try to persuade me not to do it," and she sighed, and looked wistfully out into the moonlight again. It was a sore trial to this young Christian that her mother, who had been so much of a companion to her all her life, did not sympathize with her in this great new joy.

"Let me see," said Adelaide, going back to her planning. "Lettie said something about the busy season, and not being able to get away from the workroom. I think I could manage that, however. I'll go to see Mrs. Harbison the first thing in the morning, and arrange it. Nellie Forrester is out of work for a while now on account of Madame Lee's illness, and I shouldn't wonder a bit if she would be only too glad to go in and sew in Lettie's place while she's gone. She was feeling quite badly at losing so much time the other day when I talked with her. And I'll tell Mrs. Harbison, if she's rushed just now, that she can let my dresses wait a while. I shall not need much, anyway, if I'm to stay at home. By the way, there's the new gingham I had made for travelling; it was nearly done when I was there yesterday. Mamma really hates it, though I don't see why, as it's very neat and pretty; but there's no need for me to dress in something mamma dislikes, and I wouldn't have bought it except for the sake of making those Corning girls feel that their brown sateens would be plenty good enough to wear. I believe I'll tell Lettie that if she's to go to the convention in my place, she must just take the dress, and wear it for me; for that is its legitimate purpose, and it will be disappointed if it has to stay at home;" and Adelaide laughed softly to herself as she laid her head once more on the pillow and tried to compose herself to sleep. And her friends, if they could have known that this strange girl was actually gleeful over the surrender of the thing she wanted more than all others, would have wondered at her.

It was very hard work to stop thinking that night and go to sleep; but the peace in her heart quieted her, and after a little she was asleep.

There was too much excitement about the carrying out of the new plans the next morning for Adelaide to have much time to think of her own lost pleasure. She had resolved to say nothing to her friends about the matter until she had perfected her arrangements and was sure that they would not fail. As she was a young woman accustomed to doing exactly as she pleased with her own, she anticipated no opposition further than much talk and persuasion, against which she felt that she would be able to stand, though she dreaded the ordeal, and meant to put it off as long as possible.

Immediately after breakfast the pony and phaeton came to the door, and Adelaide started out to prepare the way for the carrying out of her sacrifice. She drove first to the dressmaker's.

"She will be the very hardest stone of all to roll away," meditated Adelaide, as she touched the pony with the tip of the whip to hurry him up, "unless—it may be I shall have trouble with Lettie herself."

Mrs. Harbison came into her stuffy little parlor with a flustered face. She supposed that Miss Ashton had come to hurry up her work. It was therefore with surprise and relief that she listened to Adelaide's proposition. It had been some weeks since Mrs. Harbison had found time for a thought save about ruffles and buttons and plaits; but she proved that she had a human heart when she heard of Lettie's mother and her desire to see her; at least, she allowed herself to feel sympathy for the girl when she heard that Adelaide could suggest a substitute for her in the workroom.

"Very well; I will see Miss Forrester immediately," said Adelaide, as she took her departure, "and let you know in a short time whether she can come. And you need not trouble to hurry my dresses; for I have changed my plans somewhat, and think I shall not need them quite so soon."

"Now," said Adelaide, as she took up the reins once more. "I must pray all the way to Nellie Forrester's that she may be able to take this place;" and all the short drive was filled with earnest petition from this young, loving heart.

A Happy Morning's Work

NELLIE Forrester stood by the open window, disconsolately drumming on the sill, when the pony stopped before the door of her boarding-house, and Adelaide stepped out of the phaeton and rung the bell. Nellie Forrester's sky just now was overcast by some very black clouds, to which she could see no silver lining. She was out of work, and hopelessly so. Her former employer had been taken suddenly ill, and all her work had been sent home unfinished. Besides, her work had had none of the best reputation in her well days; and, busy season though it was, her girls had not been in demand. Nellie was a good, faithful worker; but she had been in the place only a short time, and had therefore tried in vain thus far to secure a situation. Her scanty store of dollars was fast diminishing, and she realized fully that even this miserable boarding-house would soon be beyond her means.

"If I could only get a chance to try somewhere," she said despairingly, "I'm sure I could show them good work"— Then she glanced into the street, and saw the pony. It never occurred to her that Adelaide's visit could have anything to do with her. Miss Ashton was a far-distant star, whom she had met at a sociable of the Christian Endeavor Society which she had joined on coming to the city. She had talked with Miss Ashton a few minutes, and thought her pleasant, and not nearly so haughty as her clothes looked. She admired her from afar; but this morning things looked too dark for her even to care for the bow of greeting that she usually tried to get. So she stepped back into the shadow of the curtain, wondering a little bitterly what the girl with the pony would do if she had to face the world and fight for a living. It was not until the parlor door swung open, and the voice of the slovenly maid said, "She's in here," that it entered her mind that the call might be for her.

Half an hour afterward Adelaide again stepped into her carriage and started the lazy pony from his dreams, while Nellie Forrester stood smiling at her from the door. There was a great silver rift in the black cloud now, and the bright morning sun was beginning to shine through, and it promised a glorious day.

"I declare, how little it takes to make people happy!" said Adelaide to herself; "and how much there is to make them miserable! I wonder whether there are any other unhappy members of our society. I mean to try to find out, and see whether I can help to make them happy. I'll take that for my work this summer. Now for poor little Annie Mould. I'm afraid it will bring consternation to her to think of her sister's going away. I wish she might go too. But it would be too hard a trip for so short a time. My! I wish I had a great deal of money to do some things I can think of." Then the pony was stopped once more.

Annie Mould sat by the window making buttonholes in some very coarse cloth. Adelaide felt, as she entered the dark, hot little room, that those buttonholes would have been so much more bearable if they had been on pretty material. Annie Mould had a pain in her side, which showed in the sharp pucker on her forehead; for though it was still early morning, she had been at her work for several hours, to make up for lost time the day before, when the pain had forced her to succumb entirely. Adelaide mentally resolved that this state of things should cease just as soon as she could manage it; and after a minute or two more of conversation about nothing in particular, she suddenly resolved that it should cease immediately.

"How many more of those have you to do?" she said, dashing into her subject.

Annie nodded wearily toward a great pile of similar ugly garments.

"All those, and they're to be called for at six this evening. I'm sure I don't know whether I can do it or not. Lettie can't get home to help me to-night. She has to work all the evening. I was so bad yesterday I couldn't take a stitch."

Adelaide arose with decision, and began to bundle the things together, taking the work from the astonished girl's fingers, and talking all the while, so that Annie could not object.

"I know where I can get these done, and I want you to come with me and take a little ride. I have something very important to talk with you about, and I can't talk here with you working so hard. Don't say anything now; but just be good, and do as you're told." Then followed a burst of the bright, witty remarks such as this girl knew how to make, keeping

the tired invalid in a maze of laughter till the
tears actually rolled down her cheeks. Annie
made some feeble protests, but at last surren-
dered herself to the delights of the occasion.
To have the dreadful work taken from her
aching fingers, and actually to be going on a
ride, was a wonderful experience. Adelaide
soon had her seated in the carriage, the great
bundle of work at her feet, and the pony
travelling as fast as he could amble back to
Nellie Forrester's boarding-place. That young
woman, having caught a glimpse of the carriage at the door, came into the hall, so that
Adelaide was not hindered in her errand.

"Nellie, can you make nice buttonholes?"
she questioned breathlessly.

"Beautiful ones," responded Nellie, with
sparkling eyes. "I served a two years' appren-
ticeship, doing that and nothing else. I can
make them fast too."

"Good!" exclaimed Adelaide. "I knew God
had put the thought of coming to you into my
heart. I want to get these all done by five
o'clock to-night, when I will call for them. I'll
pay you whatever you say. Do you think you
have time to finish them?" and she looked
anxiously at the other girl while she opened
the bundle and took an inventory of its con-

tents. Nellie assured her that she would be able to finish all by five o'clock, and Adelaide ran back to the carriage delighted.

"Now, Annie," she said, "the buttonholes are an assured fact, and I'm going to take you a little drive into the country, to bring some color into those white cheeks."

When the phaeton was trundling smoothly along some of the more quiet, shaded streets, Adelaide cautiously unfolded her plan, finding in the unselfish sister a grateful and delighted ally to her plotting. In spite of the shortness of that drive, it was nearly half-past eleven when they returned, and Annie was established on the bed and made comfortable to take a nap.

Adelaide paused on the curbstone to take breath and look at her watch. Would she have time to see Lettie and finish her work before lunch? Yes, if all went well; but there was no time to lose.

Lettie came from her work quite flurried when she heard that Miss Ashton was waiting to see her.

That interview was to Adelaide at once the most remarkable, the most trying, and the happiest of the four.

Lettie could not understand at first,—was dull of comprehension even to stupidity for a while; then, as it began to dawn upon her, she would have none of it, would not allow the sacrifice; and at last, when the whole plan, with all the difficulties taken out of the way, and everything made plain and easy for her bewildered, happy feet, finally burst upon her, she broke down utterly, and cried.

"You are like Jesus Christ, Miss Ashton. No one but himself, or one who had his Spirit, would think of doing a wonderful thing like that. I had begun to think he had forgotten Annie and me, but now I am ashamed."

Adelaide felt that she had rich reward already for all her sacrifice. She sent Lettie in a flutter of happy tears over the gift of the pretty gingham dress back to the workroom.

"We are just sisters, you know, children of the same Father," she had said; "and you need not take it as a gift. Between sisters things are not counted so. I shall not need the dress now; and if you can make use of it, it belongs to you. Our earthly possessions are all gifts of our Father anyway, and I think he would prefer that you should have that. You are nearly my size, and can easily make it fit you."

A few more words as to final arrangements Adelaide had with Mrs. Harbison, and then went home hungry and weary, having deliberately put away from herself all possibility of the trip to Montreal, but yet happy in spite of it.

In the joy of giving others pleasure she forgot utterly for the time her own great sacrifice. There might come a time for her to feel her own disappointment, but it was not now.

Let Not Thy Left Hand Know

IT soon became necessary for Adelaide to tell
her mother that she had decided not to go to
Montreal.

"Not going!" exclaimed her mother. "Why,
Adelaide, what in the world do you mean?
Have the rest given it up?"

"No, mamma."

"Then, what is the explanation of this
strange freak? Don't you like the arrangements? Are you tired of this constant meeting-
going? Perhaps you are coming back to your
senses again, and will be willing to go to Bar
Harbor now, though I must confess I don't
disapprove of this expedition nearly so much
as I did of the one last year. It sounds much
better to go to Montreal on a summer trip
than to New York City. Besides, the Burtons

are going. They will give tone to the party. The Burtons are still planning to go, are they not?"

"Yes, mamma," Adelaide answered, lowering her eyes, and her cheeks reddening a trifle. It was no small part of her sacrifice that she was not to enjoy the pleasure of carrying out plans made by herself and Harold and Enid Burton. "And I'm not tired of the meetings, either," she added. "You must never think so. I love the work more than I did when I came home from New York a year ago. It is for that reason I have given up the pleasure of going. There is some one else who needs to go this time more than I."

"Adelaide! This is absurdity of fanaticism. I'm sure I never supposed my daughter would turn out one of that detestable class. Don't you see how ridiculous you are? You can't go around the world finding some one who would like your things, and giving them all away. The world is full of people who would doubtless like to take a vacation. You can't spread your vacation around to humanity in this silly fashion."

"But listen, mamma, let me tell you this girl's story."

"No, I don't care to hear the story," replied her mother coldly. "Anybody can get up a sentimental story. You are entirely too soft-hearted. No story can justify you in this absurd performance. Of course you are old enough to do as you please with your own; but I warn you that if you keep on in the way you have begun, you will ruin all your prospects in life."

"O mamma! you forget that life lasts forever; and if I am pleasing Jesus Christ, I can't be ruining my prospects for life in heaven."

"Nonsense!" said her mother sharply. "One has to look out for this life a little also, you'll find. By and by, when your young life is gone, and you get over your infatuation with this society, you will blame me for not interfering now. Besides, it sounds very irreverent to me to hear you speak as you did just now. This is what I have been afraid of with these meetings. One grows entirely too familiar with sacred things, and gets to speaking of them in ordinary, careless conversation. Now do be persuaded, my dear, and give up this queer notion."

Then Mrs. Ashton launched into a most eloquent appeal, to which her daughter listened quietly, patiently, only shaking her head at the close, however, and saying a little sadly, "I'm sorry not to please you, mamma, but I feel sure I'm doing right to give this up. Please don't urge me any more."

Mrs. Ashton retired to her room soon after to think the matter over. If Adelaide really would not go, perhaps it might be made to appear to her fashionable friends that she had given up her interest in the expedition. Perhaps the girl might be won back to her former gay life. The Burtons' going was a bitter pill for her to swallow, however. They were very rich and cultured people, and a wedding with Harold Burton and Adelaide as the central figures was a pleasant thing to contemplate. There was one, just one, alleviating thought. The Burtons were such grave, religious, almost fanatical, people, that Adelaide's sacrifice might go a great way toward winning favor for her in the young man's eyes. This mother would take care that he heard of the matter, at least.

One more attempt she made to change Adelaide's purpose, allowing Lettie Mould's story to be told in full this time, and rather drawing out her daughter's intentions with regard to the care of the sick sister. Adelaide was still firm in her resolve. It was of no use to reason; therefore, if the mother was to make this matter appear well to her dear world, she must be possessed of all the facts. Her attitude was so changed that Adelaide was puzzled over the matter, and begged her mother not to let any of her young friends know of the matter, as they would trouble her with questions and regrets, and she wished to keep the matter quiet as long as possible.

Mrs. Ashton pondered the matter, a satisfied smile growing on her face as a plan formulated itself in her mind. She would have made Adelaide a present of the money to go if she could have afforded it; but it would take quite a little sum to replace the trip Adelaide was so ruthlessly giving away, and there were numerous troublesome expenses that must be met this month. She could not do it without borrowing, and that she would not do. Adelaide, she knew, had put every extra cent of her own money into the fund for sending delegates. Now, how to make this matter appear in the right light, that Adelaide's sacrifice might shine out without having people wonder why Adelaide could not go, and send Lettie Mould also if she wanted to, was Mrs. Ashton's task. She did not wish the Burtons to feel that she was not well enough off to give her daughter any number of trips to Montreal. The thought of poor Annie brought a smile to her face. What could be more beautiful, praiseworthy, and sacrificing than for Adelaide to stay to take care of Annie Mould?

Mrs. Ashton dressed herself with care to pay a call that she owed to Mrs. Burton. Seated in the Burton's cool, dark parlor, it afforded her no little satisfaction to discover between the portières at the farther end of the long library, beside the massive oak desk, a pair of russet-clad feet, and part of a coat sleeve and hand, which undoubtedly belonged to Harold, who must be sitting there writing. Mrs. Ashton's voice was clear and penetrating. She knew how to make her words heard distinctly in an adjoining room on occasion, without seeming to endeavor to do so. It did not require much management to bring the conversation around to the subject of the convention. By some skilful engineering, of which Mrs. Ashton was entirely capable, Mrs. Burton was moved to ask some questions concerning Adelaide's plans. Mrs. Burton did not realize that the question she asked was a natural outcome of Mrs. Ashton's last remark. She supposed she asked it because she was interested in the bright young girl, who was such a favorite with both her daughter and her son.

Mrs. Ashton's face became suddenly sad as she replied, "O Mrs. Burton, that dear child has upset all her plans. I'm sure I don't know how she is going to bear the sacrifice; but she is determined, and seems very brave about it. She does not want her young friends to know of it yet,"—here the lady lowered her voice decidedly, but gave to each word a distinctness and penetration that carried it straight to the ears of the young man in the other room,—"but I'm sure she'd not mind my telling you, she thinks so much of you, and you will keep her secret for her. She is not going to Montreal. She has discovered a couple of poor young things who are struggling along, whose mother lives in Montreal, and they are breaking their hearts to see her. Adelaide has made up her mind to send one of them in her place. The other sister is quite ill, and Adelaide has promised to take the girl's place in caring for her sister during her absence. Of course, if it were not for that last fact, and Adelaide's feeling so strongly that this is her work, I should insist that she go with the girl; for I could not bear to have her give it all up, in spite of the fact that she has given nearly all her pocket-money to the delegate fund. But she seems quite enthusiastic about the sacrifice, and I hardly dare to attempt to interfere with such a spirit. The dear child will come to feel it, I know, however, when the others go without her," and the mother sighed in a pathetic, satisfied way.

Mrs. Burton expressed much regret that Adelaide was not to be of the convention party, saying that her two young people would be deeply grieved, and praising the beautiful, Christlike spirit of the girl, much to the mother's satisfaction. She asked many questions, too, about the two Mould sisters, which were answered as well as Mrs. Ashton was able to answer. When the caller finally took leave, it was with a sense of having accomplished her mission. Surely the young man in the library must have heard the conversation, and she felt very certain that the hand on the desk had ceased to write during the latter part of her call.

And so, while Adelaide was quietly planning to keep her little sacrifice and disappointment from the others, partly for Lettie's sake and partly for her own, until the day of departure, her mother had spread the news to the ears that, more than all others, she would prefer should not hear it for another week yet.

5

A Comrade in Service

THE DAYS went by rapidly, but none too fast
for Adelaide. She was glad when the morning
for starting came. The intervening time had
been quite a strain upon her. Although she had
succeeded in her effort to keep the knowledge
of her change of plans from nearly all the
others of the party, still every day had brought
to her realizations of what she was giving up.
Then, too, the mother of the girl she had
promised to look out for had to be told, and
the girl herself, and Cora, her friend who was
to chaperon in her place; and there were
exclamations and commiserations and praises
to be borne, until Adelaide's heart was fairly
sick, and she wished that no one need know
until it was all over. Her only help was to keep
busy; and she plunged into work with such

good will, helping every one with plans and preparations, that they never suspected that she was not going.

At last the morning came which she longed for and rather dreaded. It would have been her pleasure not to go to the station with the others of the society, but rather to have stayed quietly at home until they were gone. But on Lettie's account that could not be. She was a new girl among them, and timid. This must be made a pleasant journey for her if the Master was to be pleased. Some words might be said that would wound Lettie's sensitive nature, and make the pleasure that she was having a burden instead, unless the way was prepared by a few words to this one and that one. Adelaide took up her cross, and went to speak those words. Just a gentle, "Nellie, will you be especially kind to Miss Mould during this journey? I want her to have a very happy time;" and, "Edwin, I wish you would look out for any wants Miss Mould may have. Do it for Jesus' sake, won't you?" A few such words were spoken to the ones that she knew might be forgetful or slighting or cold in their demeanor toward the girl. Tom Satterlee, the Burtons, and a few other friends she knew needed no reminders. They were always on the lookout for cups of cold water to be given "in His name."

Adelaide's heart almost misgave her as she passed Harold Burton on the platform, receiving his bow, which somehow bespoke a pleasant intimacy, and noting the lightening of eyes and face in a grave, sweet smile at her approach. It was worth something to have a friendship with such a young man. What pleasant times with this friend would not she lose by her self-denial!

Lettie Mould was undeniably frightened when she came to the station. She had just left poor Annie looking sick and weak. Perhaps she ought not to go, after all. The tears were scarcely dried from their parting. Then the crowd on the platform brought sudden consternation to her. Must she face them all? Must she take that terribly long journey in their company? They would all know that she was to take their favorite's place, and she would have nothing but cold glances in consequence. The dainty gray gingham that made her look so neat and pretty seemed suddenly to have Adelaide's name written all over it. Her face grew red, her heart beat fast, and her eyes were dim with unshed tears. She did not in the least know whom she was looking at or what she was going to do next, until Adelaide's arm was wound lovingly about her, and she said, "Miss Mould, I want you to know my friend Cora better. You and she must get well acquainted during this trip."

Adelaide had seen the frightened look in Lettie's face, and with her rare tact found little ways to make her feel at her ease. All the time until the train started she kept that protecting arm about the girl, and no chance was she given for hearing others wail over Adelaide's departure, for the conversation was always skilfully managed. Indeed, even at the station Adelaide managed to keep her secret pretty well; and not until the delegation was well under way did some of its members discover that she was not in their midst. Well for her plans that her mother had chosen the Burton family to whom to confide her daughter's secret, rather than some others in the church.

No time did this girl give herself for looking after the departing train, or lingering over remembrances of last year's starting. She could not even bear to sing the parting hymn, "God be with you till we meet again." The tears were too dangerously near the surface; so she slipped through the crowd unobserved, and walked rapidly down the street to the house where the lonely sister Annie lived. She would see whether people could forget themselves in doing something for others; so, with a prayer in her heart for help and courage, she pressed back the tears, and gave herself up to making Annie have a happy day.

The evening came at last, and Adelaide sat alone by the window, in the cool, dark parlor. She had turned out the lights herself; for there was no one else about just now, and the moon-light streamed in across the room, and was softer than the gaslight. Her mother and Mrs. Satterlee had gone out together in search of ice-cream and recreation at some church festival near by; but Adelaide was weary with her day, and wanted some time to herself to think things over: so she had declined their most urgent invitation to accompany them, and was alone.

Her thoughts were not altogether happy ones. She was disappointed in herself. Was she sorry she had done this thing? Was it pride alone that made her think the friends at the station did not care for her so much as she had hoped, because she had been able so easily to slip away without their knowledge? Was it wounded pride that brought that bitter pang when she remembered the glimpse she had caught of Harold Burton's face while one of the girls was telling him in sorrowful tones how she was not to be of the party? She had looked for an expression of disappointment there; but there had not been much,—only a few words which had sounded to her like polite surprise, and then he had changed the subject. Perhaps there was no reason for her to expect more of him; but he had seemed so good a friend, and in spite of herself she felt hurt. It was evident she was allowing herself to expect too much, and her cheeks glowed hot in the darkened room.

In the midst of her thoughts there came a step that made her start. It was a manly, familiar step, but belonged to one whom she supposed to be many miles away by this time. Could there be another step so like his?

He paused by the door a moment, and, seeing no one about, came on to the parlor, and stood a moment by the door, peering into the shadowed corners of the room.

Adelaide's heart stood still, and her breath came slowly; then her presence of mind came back, and she quietly rose by the window. The soft rustle of her dress attracted his attention just as he was about to go back to the door-bell for aid in finding what he wanted. He came across the room now, and took her hand in a warm, firm grasp.

"Adelaide!"

There was so much in his tone as he uttered her name, that though she tried hard to control her own voice, it would tremble as she said, "Why, Harold! I thought you were gone"—she began. "Did you think I could go without you?" he asked, bending down,—and then, "Sit down, Adelaide. I have something to tell you."

So in the moonlight there was told her a story that made all the sadness of her heart melt away, and there was so much of this story that he almost forgot to explain how it was that he discovered that she was not going.

"But, Adelaide," he said by and by, when time had slipped away so that they began to fear that the people from the festival might soon be coming home, "when I heard what a beautiful thing you were going to do, I longed to help you in your plan somehow. I could not take any credit to myself for staying at home, because I did not want to go unless you were there to enjoy it with me; so it would be no real self-denial to give up my trip. But I could use the money in some way that would please the Master. I thought of sending Annie Mould with her sister, but found upon inquiring of their landlady, who thinks a great deal of the two girls, that Annie was not physically able to take the journey, and that the thing the girls and their mother wanted most in life was to bring the mother here to live with them. It took a good deal of planning to bring it all about; but I managed it all at last. My trip to Montreal goes to bring the mother, with her goods and chattels, down here when Lettie comes back. A letter containing the money and a full explanation is probably now in her hands. I had Tom Satterlee take charge of it, and he is to give it in such a way that she need never know where it comes from. Then if there is anything else to be looked out for, he will see to it, and telegraph me if necessary. Father found out about it, and wanted to have his share in the work; so the little cottage on Rose Lane is put in order, and they can have it for a very low rent, merely nominal. Father did not dare give it for nothing, lest their feelings should be hurt."

"O Harold," said Adelaide softly, her eyes shining in the moonlight, "what wonderful things you have done! and oh, how happy I am!"

They would have talked all night, perhaps,

had they not been interrupted. Voices were heard.

"Your mother is coming, Adelaide; I want to ask her to-night. May I? I want to feel that you are surely my own."

A little later that same evening Mrs. Ashton sat in her room, and surveyed herself with satisfaction. "Thank fortune, Adelaide is safe at last!" she said to herself. "I knew I could manage it if I put my mind to it."

And Adelaide, in the quiet of her own room, opened the leaves of her Bible, and read, "I will lead them in paths that they have not known." She smiled as she read, and then knelt down to thank her heavenly Father for his wonderful ways with her.

Some Peculiar People
in Our Society

THE SOCIETY of which I write was organized some eight years ago in a brisk little village in the South. It sailed into existence with flying colors, having at the start forty active members and sixteen associate. All the necessary, and some unnecessary, committees were formed; they set to work with a right good will, and for a time all things looked prosperous.

Now, there were in that society people of all sorts and conditions. There were people who were easily hurt; people who always wanted to manage; people who were never satisfied; people who feared the society was doing more harm than good by running itself this way or that; people who thought there were some in the society who did not belong there, and others who held the same opinion concerning them; people young and people old, for the society was not limited in regard to age; indeed, there were some older members who needed the society as much as did the younger ones. In short, the different types of humanity were all there, and each one with some crotchet of his own; but there were so many different crotchets that the people who owned them had ceased to be called queer for them, and so it is merely about the three most peculiar members that I have to tell. They were the Pray-er, the Peacemaker, and the Man-who-was-willing-to-give-up.

The Pray-er was a rather oldish young woman, with great thoughtful brown eyes, who wore a plain face and a plainer dress. Not that she was the only one in the society who prayed. By no means. They were good, earnest members, most of them, who meant to keep their pledge, and tried much of the time to do so; but she was one who was wont to take her every wish or doubt to the feet of the Master, and ask his will concerning it. Her townspeople said Miss Fairfield was a little peculiar, but just as good as could be. All loved her; and it was a noticeable fact that whenever one was in serious doubt or dire perplexity he would go to the Pray-er for counsel, so that in the minds of some few she came to be also called a counsellor.

The Peacemaker was the wife of the Man-who-was-willing-to-give-up. They were a young couple who had consecrated their all to the Master's use. "I wonder, dear," said the Peacemaker to her husband one day, when they had been having a troubled talk together concerning an irritation that had sprung up between certain touchy members of the society, who were by some voted "queer" and "cranky," "I wonder whether we are cranks too," and she sighed a thoughtful, troubled little sigh. Then they both laughed.

Now, about the time for the third semi-annual election of officers, there arose a dispute among the members of our society as to who should be greatest. The nominating committee had been carefully chosen by the retiring president with a view to wise arrangements of committees and officers. As the pastor of the church was one of the number, he felt that all would move on smoothly. But when the committee appeared, and announced as their candidate for president the Man-who-was-willing-to-give-up, there was deep silence, and an ominous scowl on the faces of several members; for, strange to say, some few were jealous of this man.

We accepted the report; of course we did: it was a way we had in our society, of always accepting without a murmur whatever was done in our business meetings, and then proceeding to growl about it and stir up a fuss as soon as the meeting was concluded. This was no exception. The Man-whose-feelings-were-always-getting-hurt had expected, fully expected, to be made president himself, owing to his having been one of the first movers in the organization of the society. He had been looking for it each term, and it really seemed to him to be his turn in the natural order of things. His feelings, however, would not have been quite so badly hurt if he had been made vice-president, perhaps, or secretary, or treasurer, or even a chairman of one of the three principal committees; but he was merely a sub-member of the flower committee,—a committee that seemed to him to be a great nuisance and of very little use in the world. He went home in ill-humor, and glowered and sulked around for a week, no one knowing what was the matter. At last he wrote a curt request for dismissal from the society, and handed it to the secretary, to be read at the next business meeting. The secretary was a novice, and did not know that the letter should have been handed to the lookout committee; but he whispered it about here and there that such a letter had been given him, and the story got afloat that the Man-whose-feelings-were-always-getting-hurt was hurt again, and there were various theories as to the cause. Some said he had better be let go, that such a man was more harm than good to them; and the story grew, and came to the ears of the man in question, which made his feelings sorer than ever.

Meanwhile, the prayer-meeting committee came together, and omitted to ask two young members to lead meetings; whereupon said members concluded that they were not wanted, and one of them proceeded to stay away from the church, while the other took a very back seat, and kept his lips tightly closed, apparently forgetting that his pledge was made to the Lord, and not to his fellow-members.

This committee also offended another member who, when asked to lead, requested to be given a consecration meeting; and upon being told that all such were already arranged for, declared he would lead none at all if he could not lead that. Whereupon the indignant member of the prayer-meeting committee who was talking with him, having already had her patience tried to its utmost by two or three other members, told him in very plain language that one who was so proud as that was not fit to lead a consecration meeting, or any other. Which plain truth, it will be seen, did not effectually cure the pride of the young man, who joined the ranks of the pledge-breakers for some time thereafter, and kept his mouth sealed in meeting.

The music committee, in their ardent desire to do their duty, not finding sufficient opportunity in the social gatherings held occasionally, decided to take in charge the music of the prayer-meetings, and better it if they could. They had heard that a young lady who had recently come among them was a fine performer; and it was thought that she would be willing to take charge of the organ and lead the singing if she were asked. The only question was how to get rid of the girl who had always held that place. They talked it over so much that it presently became town talk; and the Girl-who-had-always-played-the-organ heard of it, and settled the difficult question by herself remaining at home for several Sabbath evenings. It was even rumored that the Girl-who-was-always-willing-to-play-the-organ said that the Girl-who-had-always-played-the-organ dragged horribly, and did not know a thing about the stops, and she was sure *she* could not sing at all with such playing. Upon hearing this from several intimate friends, with the varied interpretations that the individual intonations and gestures and the originality of these friends put upon the words, the Girl-who-had-always-played-the-organ spent a day or two in secret tears, then indignantly declined to have anything more to do with the organ or the choir or the church or the Young People's Society of Christian Endeavor, and betook herself temporarily to another church. Of course the members took sides immediately, her friends declaring that it was a shame, and that they would not sing a word if the playing was done by the Girl-who-was-willing-to-play-the-organ. So in God's house they would sit dumb, when the Father above was listening for his "little human praise," and missing it from those angry children of his. The enemies of the Girl-who-had-always-played-the-organ were glad, and immediately established the new organist, saying that they had always thought the old one dragged, and did not know how to play, anyway.

Then the financial committee, which was a new institution with the incoming term of office, decided to put its finger into the pie. They held meeting after meeting, scribbling forms for a pledge-card, by which method they hoped to be able to roll the money into the treasury, which at the time of their coming into office contained the large sum of seventeen cents. At last they presented their plan to the society.

Now, there was no doubt in the minds of any of us that the method of raising money by individual pledges was the correct way to do things; but when the pledge-card suggested by the financial committee was read, and it was found that only one-quarter of all money received was devoted to benevolence by it, there began loud murmurs and long discussions, and the business meeting protracted itself far into the evening. Some thought the money should all be given to benevolence, while the others thought it all belonged to the society for its own expenses. Of this number were the entire social committee, who had in mind entertainments that would require elaborate costumes. There was still a third class,— but very small,—who thought that a certain small portion of the money pledged should belong to the society for running expenses, while the remainder should be set apart for benevolence. The debate was a hot one; and so many sharp criticisms were made upon the wording of the card, that the writer of it, after defending it in several very long speeches, became exceedingly angry, and resigned.

Now, the president, the Man-who-was-willing-to-give-up, was opposed to the division of money that had been made in the pledge-cards. He thought more ought to be given to benevolence, and less to running expenses. He had even asked permission to speak upon the subject, and had made a concise little speech, which ought to have carried conviction to all hearts; but some of his sentences had been almost too true for the peace of mind of those who were on the other side, and had cut sharply. When the president saw how matters stood, that the financial committee had taken offence at what had been said, and that not only one member had resigned, but the other four were on the eve of doing the same thing, he arose, and proved his right to be called the Man-who-was-always-willing-to-give-up.

"Dear friends," he said, "let us not be too hasty about this matter, and do in a heat that of which we shall repent. There is no need for this friend to resign his position, merely because the recommendation of his committee has been criticised somewhat. Perhaps, after all, his way is right. For my own part, if I have said anything that has seemed unlovely, I most sincerely ask pardon, and I hope that some compromise will be made, or that the plan proposed will be tried for a time at least, that we may see whether it will work. Let us remember that we are all children of the same King, and that he has commanded us to love one another. I am willing to give up my preference in the matter, should it seem best to the rest of the members."

That was the first drop of oil poured upon the troubled waters, which, nevertheless, continued to heave and roll as the days went by, and each of the various irritations in the society became more grievous, and were added to by other things, many of them small in themselves, but exceedingly large when considered in the light of the larger troubles to which they had attached themselves.

"Our president is peculiar," said one member to another after that long business meeting, as he thoughtfully wended his way home. "Who would have thought he would have so gracefully given up, after that sharp speech he made on the other side? I declare, there was a good deal of force in what he said about giving the larger part of our money to the Lord. I don't know but he was in the right after all; but I never would have let people think I was willing to give up either way if it had been my case."

"Yes, he is rather queer about some things," replied the other after a pause; "and so is his wife, for the matter of that. She seems to think of things that no one else does. Now, to-night she came to me, and asked me right out, pointblank, whether I wasn't willing to forgive Matthews, and go and invite him to the social gathering that is to be held at my house this week; and when I tried to tell her how meanly he had treated me, and how sneaking he had been about it all, she just said, 'Yes, I know he's rather hard to get along with; but we have to forgive, you know, and I suppose we all do things that other people don't like. Jesus Christ died for him, you know; and therefore if he can get along with him, we ought to be able to, with his help.'"

"H'm! What did you say?"

"Well,—I—I—I didn't say much of anything. The fact is, I don't know but she's more than half right about it. Anyway, I'd treat Matthews all right if he should come to the sociable, and that's going a good way. He ought to be thankful for that. Of course I can't go so far as to invite him; but if he's a mind to come, all right."

"He won't come unless you invite him."

"Why not? He's been invited from the pulpit. They invited every one."

"But he knows how you feel toward him."

"Well, if he's such a goose as to stay away, I can't help it."

Then these two members went thoughtfully on their way.

The next day the Peacemaker started out on a self-appointed mission. She went to the store where Mr. Matthews was clerk, and, after buying some thread, said to him, as he was doing it up, "By the way, Mr. Matthews, are you to be at the sociable on Friday evening?"

"Why, I don't know," answered the young man. "Where is it to be held?"

"At the Appletons'. Don't you remember the notice?"

"Oh!" he said, his face suddenly darkening. "No, I think not; I do not think I can be spared from the store that evening."

"Oh, that would be a pity! I mean to ask Mr. Sheldon myself whether he cannot spare you. You see, I have a friend who is coming to spend a few days with me, and I want her to meet you. I know you will like her, and the only free evening is that of the sociable. I am sure you could come if you would try."

The young man appeared embarrassed between his desire to please the Peacemaker and meet her friend, and his intention not to go to the sociable.

"Well, the fact is," he said at last, after a moment's hesitation, "I don't like to go to that house. You see, Appleton doesn't like me very much, and he hasn't treated me well for a long time. I'd like to meet your friend, but you see how it is."

The Peacemaker never told any one but her husband what was said during the long, earnest talk that followed, but there was a more sober look on young Matthews's face, and he went to the sociable on Friday evening; moreover, young Appleton and his wife shook hands with him.

It was that same week that the Pray-er, the Peacemaker, and the Man-who-was-willing-to-give-up had a little meeting all by themselves. It came about in the most natural way. The Pray-er called upon the Peacemaker, and, before she left, the Peacemaker's husband came in. Talk drifted into society matters and the troubles and constant fallings out. The question came up, "What can be done?"

"We must be ready to compromise with them, to surrender so much of our own way as we conscientiously can, and then go ahead. That is all that I see can be done," said the Man-who-was-willing-to-give-up, passing his hand wearily over his eyes, and then looking in a perplexed way at the toe of his right boot, as though that ought to be able to help him out.

"Perhaps a little might be done by quietly bringing these people together, and leading them to look one upon the other's side of the question. A little word sometimes will cool people down when it comes from an outsider who can have no possible bias either way," suggested his wife, looking thoughtfully into the fire.

"We must pray," said Miss Fairfield; and the words came from her quiet lips with such tremendous force that both the Peacemaker and her husband felt the need of prayer as they had never felt it before, and both looked up with a sudden lighting of the eyes and softening of the faces.

So they prayed. Yes, right there in the parlor, during an afternoon formal call; at least, that was what it started out to be, for the Pray-er had never been well acquainted with the president and his wife before. Miss Fairfield's card-case was laid aside upon the floor, and she forgot for the moment where she was, so intent was she upon the one thought,—their society and its immediate needs.

"Let us pray now," had the president said. "We ought to have remembered that before. Will you join with us right here? There can be no better time." And they had knelt and poured out their hearts in petition for a blessing upon the members of their society of Christian Endeavor.

Yes, it was a peculiar thing to do. They were indeed a peculiar people; and of them truly it might be said, "For thou art an holy people unto the Lord thy God, and the Lord hath chosen thee to be a peculiar people unto himself."

The call lasted much longer than fashion required, for when they arose from their knees they found that the Lord had put much into their hearts to say to one another.

"Miss Edgerton thinks," said the president, "that the society is going to wreck and ruin because the members will not arise when they speak in the meetings. I dislike the idea of giving up the informality that comes to a pleasant little meeting of the size of ours when we remain seated to speak; but perhaps it would be as well to take the stumbling-block out of the way of some few, and for one or two of us to arise occasionally, letting it be felt that either way is the custom."

This was said when their hearts were softened by communion with their Saviour, and they felt willing to be all things to all men, even though they must sacrifice their own pet theories.

So it was arranged that two or three other earnest members who were always ready to help should be taken into the secret, and that at the next business meeting the president should say a few words that were in his heart about how troubled he felt lest they were getting into a rut of formalities that would lead them even farther away from Christ than they had been before their society was organized, and about his wishing that the prospering of their work might not all be outward, but that they might have a work done in their own hearts, that they might make more of their consecration meetings, and reach out farther for those who were not in the society, and were not being influenced by it at all, closing with the request that they would speak their minds freely concerning the matter, and then kneel and reconsecrate themselves and their society.

The days went by, and much praying was done by these three souls.

"See here," said the president, bringing his open Bible to his wife on the day before the next business meeting, "I have found an encouragement from the Lord for us. Surely we may claim this for ourselves, and take courage," and he held the book before her, and pointed to these words: "For thou art an holy people unto the Lord thy God: the Lord thy God hath chosen thee to be a special people unto himself, above all people that are upon the face of the earth. The Lord did not set his love upon you, nor choose you, because ye were more in number than any people; for ye were the fewest of all people; but because the Lord loved you, and because he would keep the oath which he had sworn unto your fathers, hath the Lord brought you out with a mighty hand and redeemed you."

The evening of the meeting arrived, and the programme was carried out, at least so far as those who had planned beforehand could carry it. The president spoke, and the few who had agreed to do so seconded him. Not another member spoke, and all looked surprised; but they knelt to pray with sober faces, and more than one was seen wiping his eyes when they arose. There was not much merriment as they went out. Indeed, quite a number came to the president and to the others who had seconded him, and said that they fully agreed with them, but that they had not felt worthy to speak. They supposed that they ought always to feel ready to speak or pray; but the call had been so unexpected, and it had aroused them to think that perhaps God would call some day when they were not ready.

That evening marked a new era. The consecration meetings, and indeed all other meetings, were different affairs after that from what they had been. There began gradually to be many short prayers, more short, earnest sentences spoken from the heart and from personal experience; and when Bible verses were recited, instead of being rattled off, a perfect avalanche of them, as rapidly as they could come, they seemed to be spoken more thoughtfully, as if the speaker were feeling every word that was uttered.

Then the Week of Prayer came on, and the Christian Endeavor Society was asked to take charge of part of the meetings; and when the week was over we found that we could not close, for many were asking the way to be saved, and so the work continued. Old irritations somehow fell out of notice. The Man-whose-feelings-were-always-getting-hurt forgave and forgot; the Girl-who-had-always-played-the-organ and the Girl-who-had-been-willing-to-play-it somehow became very good friends, and divided the labors of that instrument between them; and the hurt member, who had asked to be dismissed, applied for readmission, and publicly announced that he had been wrong in a good many things, and that he hoped the members would forgive him. Oh, it was indeed a wonderful time!

Professor Drummond says,—

Christianity is a fine inoculation, a transfusion of healthy blood into an anæmic or poisoned soul. No fever can attack a perfectly sound body; no fever of unrest can disturb a soul which has breathed the air or learned the ways of Christ. . . . Christ's yoke is simply his secret for the alleviation of human life, his prescription for the best and happiest method of living. . . Touchiness, in spite of its innocent name, is one of the gravest sources of restlessness in the world. Touchiness, when it becomes chronic, is a morbid condition of the inward disposition. It is self-love inflamed to the acute point, conceit *with a hair-trigger.* The cure is to shift the yoke to some other place, to let men and things touch us through some new, and perhaps as yet unused, part of our nature, to become meek and lowly in heart, while the old sensitiveness is becoming numb from want of use. It is the beautiful work of Christianity everywhere to adjust the burden of life to those who bear it, and them to it. It has a perfectly miraculous gift of healing.

Many of the members of our society had been afflicted for years with the disease of touchiness; but now, coming into the atmosphere of Jesus Christ, and learning to wear his yoke and to be "meek and lowly in heart," they found "rest unto their souls," and began to love one another and to forget old strifes.

But there came a sad time a little later. The Pray-er, the dear, loved soul who had helped us so many times, whose prayers and whose counsels we felt that we could not do without, lay down to die. Going from the heated church to her home in the cold air every evening had been too much for her delicate throat and lungs; and she had taken a severe cold, which grew into something more serious, and would not be controlled.

We gathered about her with tears, and knelt by her bedside while she uttered her last prayer for the society that she loved.

"Dear Lord," she prayed, "oh, that they may be one, even as thou, Father, and thy Son are one!" These were the last words that she spoke on earth.

As we knelt there, it seemed as though the very presence of the great God were in the room; and all our petty quarrels, envyings, and self-loves looked so small, so mean, so low, that we would fain have hid our faces, so much did we despise ourselves, and we looked with longing and covetousness upon the peaceful face before us. Oh, if we could feel the peace that belonged to her whom we had once called "strange" and "a little peculiar"! She folded her quiet hands that had always been so willing to do for others, and like a tired child fell asleep to awake in heaven. On her brow was the seal of His ownership. She was His "peculiar treasure" now, taken home to dwell with Him. She had at last seen Him for whose glorious appearing she had been so long looking, who "gave himself for us, that he might redeem us from all iniquity, and purify unto himself a peculiar people, zealous of good works." She had been lent to us to help us for a little while, and now the Lord had taken her back. We could but feel, as we looked upon her dear face for the last time, and remembered the loving, earnest, sheltered life she had lived, that indeed the promise of old, concerning enemies and dangers, had been verified for her,—that "fear and dread shall fall upon them; by the greatness of thine arm they shall be as still as a stone; till thy people pass over, O Lord, till the people pass over, which thou hast purchased. Thou shalt bring them in, and plant them in the mountain of thine inheritance, in the place, O Lord, which thou hast made for them to dwell in, in the sanctuary, O Lord, which thy hands have established."

She has passed over; but the Peacemaker and the Man-who-was-willing-to-give-up are not left to be the only peculiar people in that society. There are many Pray-ers, earnest ones too, and the whole society is struggling to belong to the "peculiar people," that we may show forth the praises of Him who has called us out of darkness into His marvellous light.

About the Author

Grace Livingston Hill is well known as one of the most prolific writers of romantic fiction. Her personal life was fraught with joys and sorrows not unlike those experienced by many of her fictional heroines.

Born in Wellsville, New York, Grace nearly died during the first hours of life. But her loving parents and friends turned to God in prayer. She survived miraculously; thus her thankful father named her Grace.

Grace was always close to her father, a Presbyterian minister, and her mother, a published writer. It was from them that she learned the art of storytelling. When Grace was twelve, a close aunt surprised her with a hardbound, illustrated copy of one of Grace's stories. This was the beginning of Grace's journey into being a published author.

In 1892 Grace married Fred Hill, a young minister, and they soon had two lovely young daughters. Then came 1901, a difficult year for Grace—the year when, within months of each other, both her father and her husband died. Suddenly Grace had to find a new place to live (her home was owned by the church where her husband had been pastor). It was a struggle for Grace to raise her young daughters alone, but through everything she kept writing. In 1902 she produced *The Angel of His Presence, The Story of a Whim,* and *An Unwilling Guest.* In 1903 her two books *According to the Pattern* and *Because of Stephen* were published.

It wasn't long before Grace was a well-known author, but she wanted to go beyond just entertaining her readers. She soon included the message of God's salvation through Jesus Christ in each of her books. For Grace, the most important thing she did was not write books but share the message of salvation, a message she felt God wanted her to share through the abilities he had given her.

In all, Grace Livingston Hill wrote more than one hundred books, all of which have sold thousands of copies and have touched the lives of readers around the world with their message of "enduring love" and the true way to lasting happiness: a relationship with God through his Son, Jesus Christ.

In an interview shortly before her death, Grace's devotion to her Lord still shone clear. She commented that whatever she had accomplished had been God's doing. She was only his servant, one who had tried to follow his teaching in all her thoughts and writing.

Don't miss these Grace Livingston Hill romance novels!